DEEP OVERSTOCK

#23: Ghosts
January 2024

> If anyone boos you offstage, that is simply applause from ghosts.
>
> *Sharon Needles*

PARA - GHOSTS

Editorial

Editors-In-Chief: Mickey Collins & Robert Eversmann

Managing Editor: Z.B. Wagman

Poetry: Timothy Arliss OBrien, Jihye Shin & Nicholas Yandell

Prose: Heather Hambley

Cover: Ghostie's Tomb by J. Remy LeStrange

Contact: editors@deepoverstock.com
deepoverstock.com

ON THE SHELVES

7   In the Attic by Coleman Stevenson

8   How to Hunt a Ghost by Callie S. Blackstone

10   Telling the Bees by KB Ballentine

11   1971 by Janis Lee Scott

14   The Supermarket Spectre by Sarah Das Gupta

15   A Triptych by RJ Equality Ingram

17   DISEMBODIMENT by Christopher Barnes

18   The Nightly Visitor by Ken Gosse

19   First Lecture in Phantomnation by Kai Broach

21   Seventeen Years by Ann Howells

22   Ghost Mask, Mask Shop, Venice, Italy by Roger Camp

23   Two Girls Watching TV by Valerie Hunter

25   Excerpts from San Narciso: Republican, Tragic & Romantic novel on Mexican National Affairs by Joe Galván

32   Pensioner of the Merchant Marine by Keith Melton

33   Haunt Me Gently by Nicholas Yandell

35   Ancestors by Lynette Esposito

36   Granny's Ghost by Sarah Das Gupta

37   What Cannot Be Changed by KB Ballentine

38   Out There by S.Z. James

41   I Summon Our Dead Sister to Our Dying Father's Bedside by Gabby Gilliam

42   THE FAMILY GHOST by Dee Allen

44   Tricks Mix by Ken Gosse

45   Sabrina by Christine Eskilson

49   Those Whose Memories I Share by Ann Howells

50   Rata Udre Udre by Mike Wilson

57   Early March by Lynette Esposito

58   Tenth Muse; or, Callisto of Lesbos by Ivy Jong

61   Proper ID Required by Karla Linn Merrifield

62   Merlin Merlot by A.A. Slaterpryce

Continued...

63	Ghost by Sophie Spisak	103	The Holiday Kitchen by Lynette Esposito
64	The Exorcism by Kara McMullen	104	The Shortest Night by KB Ballentine
73	A Way to Find You by KB Ballentine		
74	Interview with a Ghost by Timothy Arliss OBrien		
77	Sleeping In by Gabby Gilliam		
78	Miles of Ghosts by Gurupreet K. Khalsa		
79	Around the House by James B. Nicola		
80	Icicles Before Spring by Lynette Esposito		
81	Halloween Still Life With Birds by Aletha Irby		
82	NOPPERO-BO by Dee Allen		
84	Imponderable by Ann Howells		
85	Awake by Cynthia Graae		
91	You Know It's Coming by Molly O'Dell		
92	Imagined by Valerie Hunter		
94	A HAUNTED HOUSE by Sarah Das Gupta		
95	Upholstery Geist by Abbie Doll		

Letter from the Editors

Dearest Readers,

These winter months of cold are dark give us the chills and goosebumps. Or perhaps that's just the feeling of anticipation that comes when you have new prose and poetry to read.

It's been too long. Did you think we ghosted you? You certainly ghosted us and we're happy for it. Thanks to you, *Deep Overstock* is back in the flesh…or lack thereof.

Within these pages you hold are haunts both happy and sad, with a feeling of unfinished business. To open this tome is to invite the ghosts of family, friends, strangers, and even houses into your life.

Just remember that even after you close this journal, these stories will continue to stay with you, so make your peace with them as you go.

Now, as we lay *Ghosts* to rest, we ask that you resurrect classic tales of old. We ask that you send us re-tellings of tales been told, stories of classic cars, one-liners that never get old, or whatever other classic you dig up, and send them to us for our *Classics* issue before the February 28th, 2024 deadline.

Yours, the ever-present and ghostly pale,

Deep Overstock Editors

In the Attic
by Coleman Stevenson

Scavenged from the poem "Sway" by Denis Johnson

In terror I did not know
what to say. Between the bones,
grey breath, tarantella of once-feathers,
a pillow of herself, too much, it seemed,
for a skull this size. This is a story that begins
so stealthily, it's over before we know something's there.
Now the floor is opened. The bones suffer the light,
no longer love the wrestling of seed from suet,
berry from bramble. Who she was is all of us
in the sway of harmony and divergence,
sway of coyote and hyena that would have come
to eat her elsewhere. Nothing but the gradual
grinding of air could have her here. Every piece
of the world blends in. You will. I shall
now move my hands through the crevice in the wood
and scoop her out, brush away the fluff.
All moves to an end, and ends:
a hole in the floor. Ambulances. Fire-gutted cars.
Why even speak if it can't come out a poem?

How to Hunt a Ghost
by Callie S. Blackstone

Enter the graveyard.
Walk the rows.
Pause

take in names, dates,
all of it, even the things left behind
for the dead: plastic flowers,
foil whirligigs, stone angels watching,
watching.

Mausoleums, grave plates,
honor them all: death,
the great equalizer.

Yes, you must walk the rows
before you approach her.

She is in the back, hidden under
low tree branches. Few dare
to meet her beyond hubristic
teenagers and local history buffs.
Which are you?

Approach with reverence.
Her stone is covered in a pile
of florid fall leaves. Kneel.
Clear them. Take in the stone,
savor each word. *Here lies*

After you leave her,
enter your car. Drive
the surrounding roads.
There is a legend about each--
you could find her on any of them,
the woman in the red dress.

They say she has died many kinds of deaths.

The specifics are lost in any number of stories--
angered lover, lost lover, lost child, angered child.

No matter. We know she died. We know she lingers on.

You know she lingers on. You heard the stories in grade school, you grew up on them. You know she lingers on, you tell yourself, after repeating the ritual yet again, after viewing her grave, yet again, after driving these roads yet again. She lingers on

A red blur

Telling the Bees
by KB Ballentine

Do I mention you by name? Tell them
    how I lost you? Or do they already know –
your presence already humming in the hive?

This honey-colored day should be gray,
    misted and fogged as my dreams.
Or maybe not.

Maybe the sun glides over the sycamores
    and sweet gums, flecks the ferns with shade
and shine because your spirit infuses
    this place with memories of your laugh,
of your hands – careful and kind.

One gatherer mumbles past, whispering
    the tip of my ear. Maybe I shouldn't tell them.

You *are* here.

1971
by Janis Lee Scott

When my husband, Doug, and I lived on Cuesta Grade in SLO, I started dreaming about this man in a blue uniform with a name tag. This dream kept coming back, but I could never make out the name. It was a recurring dream which had a sense of urgency to it. The man appeared outside my house, usually at night, trying quietly to break in. He had little tools with him: a tiny saw to try and slice the window lock open, a pick to force front entry, and a scraper to find weak places where window and wood met. Meticulously, the man tried all his special tools while watching me. He stared in with a vacant smile. I looked back, so frightened that I couldn't move, which made me feel helpless.

This recurring dream continued when we moved to Oceanaire, closer to town. The murder of a young woman took place not long after, causing our town and our new neighborhood not to feel as safe. My friend, Mark, offered to take me by Hysen-Johnson to drop my car off since it was due for service and not too far out of Mark's way, just a couple miles from the car dealership to my house. I had just slid out of my car and handed it over, watching the mechanic's helper park it in the garage. He hopped out like a man on a mission. "Hey Mark, long time no see. How are you? I don't think we've seen each other since high school." He pointed at me. "Is this your wife? I can take her home if you've got to get back to work."

Mark looked flustered. "No, no, this is the boss's wife. Just helping get her here."

I looked at the name tag on the mechanic's helper-blue uniform. "Thanks, Jeff," Mark said. "But, I'll take her home."

Jeff moved closer to me until we were standing face to face. "Nice to meet you, but I'm not that far away, and Mark doesn't mind," I said. "Do you Mark?" I knew something didn't feel right, and I should pay attention. Jeff shook my hand, and it forced me to hold my breath. I realized he held an invoice that had my information.

He gave me a shrug and a vacant smile. "Suit yourself. Bye, Mark. Maybe we'll see each other in another ten."

Mark didn't utter a word, just waved his hand as we got in his car and pulled out of the parking lot. "There's something about that guy I don't trust," Mark said. "I'm bringing you back when the car is done if Doug isn't home."

I agreed with a nod. In my head, I'd put it all together: the blue uniform, the empty name tag, and the vacant smile. I shivered at the thought that this was my mystery man from all of those creepy dreams. Could he really jump out of my nightmares and into my waking life via a car dealership?

After meeting Jeff, I became obsessed with the murder, sitting down every morning with my coffee and newspapers, new and old. I felt like the murdered woman was sitting down with me as we went through the information, attempting to put it all together. I found out from the stack of papers that the young woman was a local, probably close to the same age as Mark. I put a coffee cup down for Alice since I felt she was near. "Alice, please sit. I brought you a coffee. Let me know when something rings true."

The phone rang. Mark sounded excited, talking fast and first. "You know that I went to school with that girl? Her body was found in her apartment, along with a suitcase and roundtrip airline ticket to San Diego. Somebody she shouldn't have trusted must've given her a ride home."

I think of my ride home invitation with an unsettled feeling. "Do you think she could have been friends with Jeff?" I asked.

"They didn't date, but they were friends. Alice always stood up for him. Even back then, he was always stirring up trouble."

And now, she has a slit throat for all of her effort, I thought to myself.

The night the second murder took place, I was alone in the house and had a nightmare. I was trying to get out of the house, away from someone. I could hear warning voices, trying to wake me, to get me moving out of the house. Maybe it was Alice or my spirit side or both. I felt the need to get out fast. I jumped out of bed, grabbed my keys, and ran for the front door (no time for a robe, purse, or shoes). I jumped in the car, and for some reason, the windows were rolled down. As the engine turned over, the assailant grabbed my arm from the window as I caught a glimpse of his nametag. My heart stopped, and lights came on. I knew that Jeff had killed a second woman because both she and Alice stood in front of the car, glowing from the high beams.

The Supermarket Spectre
by Sarah Das Gupta

I'm stacking empty shelves,
in an empty Superstore.
Between the empty spaces,
I see a strange old man
mopping the black and white floor.

Slowly the spaces are filled,
baked beans, peas and peaches
block out my view of the aisle.
Still, I hear the swish of the mop
on the shop's filthy floor.

With my empty trolley I turn,
round the end of the row.
The old man's carrying his bucket.
His uniform's a faded, dark green,
as he mutters, 'Good evening, my dear.'

My trolley's been magically filled,
with weird, outdated brands,
old-fashioned soaps and shampoos.
The man's now in the next aisle.
I notice he floats as he moves.

Peering through spaces between packets,
he is frantically washing the floor.
There's a strange green haze
hovers and shimmers around him
and the tins rattle more and more.

I hand in my keys as I finish.
The boss has heard of my ghost.
He was crushed by a falling shelf,
more than twenty years ago.
'But he still comes to work
to mop up the blood, you know.'

A Triptych
by RJ Equality Ingram

THE GHOST OF CHRISTMAS PRESENTS PAST

On our twelfth year's Christmas we tried
To find ourselves the kind of couple who
Swings but instead it became you me &
A third wheel who all but wrapped mouths
Around our ornamented curriculum vitae
Blushing we offered ourselves peppermint
Party shooters w/ a real bad name Santa's
Frosty Nipple or Vixen Didn't Get None bc
RJ got too drunk to enjoy open marriages
Too drunk to watch the busboy ask to be
Our lover bc I thought you wanted to brag
About this love that ppl want you to share
Goodwill is a warehouse full of forgotten
Christmas presents here is a shovel: now dig

THE GHOSTING OF CHRISTMAS PRESENT

Sometimes you've got to throw yourself
Out there & come in & know me better
Man like when you tried to mansplain
A Christmas Carol to a Dickens scholar
Or reinvent the way ship sails cascade
Through the river like a family of swans
I don't blame you for trying to make the
Best out of a cold holiday in the mountains
Even for underestimating unwritten poetry
Except you can be everywhere all at once
A river peppered w/ white birds flightless
Until the down falls into the cold banks
This was supposed to be a thirst trap
Instead it's a poem about moving on

THE GHOST OF CHRISTMAS YET TO CUM

The thing is I know I invited you over but
You didn't tell me that when you take your
Shirt off a pimple would be waiting for me
On your shoulder blades the kind my mom
Would pop for us when we couldn't reach
And I can't think of anything less sexy than
My mother popping strange men's pimples
Except I don't ask you to leave I pretend
It's the two of us on our honeymoon you
Shaking martinis & me in a feathered robe
We've escaped the world for long enough
I invite you over to pour my drink & when
You slide your shirt off I grab the fucker
Between my knuckles & out pops Endora

DISEMBODIMENT
by Christopher Barnes

                          n
   l   u   n
bl   e   u   nc
Invisible, nebulous continuance.

The morbid urn grief -
Haunters surge firmest lids.

Epitaphs, whispers.
       hs   rs
       h   s

The Nightly Visitor
by Ken Gosse

A lonely evening, naught in sight
but muted hue of red and blue;
the distant glare of corner's light
where few will tread the path at night.

You see a figure by the door,
a palish white, a moment's fright,
the ghost of some provincial lore—
a lonely shore on barren moor.

It's quickly gone, as if a flare
burned out before we might explore
the reason it was standing there;
we're left with nothing but its glare.

They tell me that the story's true:
a soul's despair once captured where
his love could not her love imbue—
he chose love's flame to end his rue.

First Lecture in Phantomnation
by Kai Broach

From the Oxford English Dictionary, 5th Edition © 2123):

ghost word *[gōst wərd] n. a word in a dictionary or another collection of words that is not a real word and is usually there because of a mistake*[1]

phantomnation *[ˈfantəm ˈnāSHən] n.* **1.** *Also known as ectolinguistics; the study or attempt at reproduction of the language of ghosts* **2.** *(archaic) Appearance of a phantom; illusion. A ghost word resulting from an erroneous reproduction of Alexander Pope's 1725 translation of* The Odyssey[2]

The great poems of the 21st century were written in absence. A new ancient language with a script something like the hypothetical bits of blank notebook left   splattered white with potential around   "Things fall apart; the center cannot hold"   if   a Stater bullet had gleaned it from Yeats' teeming brain   before his pen could.

The absence of the train is still the train,   air whistling into un-air the way glaciers are sea rushing into un-sea. So the ghost where a word on a page on a book of poems on   a life disappeared into   un-word became the new medium. Entropy the oldest ghost story, finally understood   as such by a poetics despairing understanding in an era when information displaced   truth. Truth   whistled in behind the   caboose but by that point you were plastered to the locomotive.

In those days, love was defined as the absence of love unmarked. Attendance spotless.   Gothic logic that something you could absent from loved you because   it kept a checkbox next to your name with its mouth open

---

[1] A living term that only exists because of the lives of dead words.
[2] "These solemn vows and holy offerings paid/To all the phantomnations of the dead."

begging   for ink, for you   to show up in that invisible way, fill the white space'   s howl.   Meanwhile, ghosts spoke in   drop-outs in   names unrolled, uncalled for. Sound waves   that shivered up the bell curve and back into the clapper. Speakers that oozed themselves   through the woofer rather than utter another untruth. Boxes whited open, spilling silence.

Like the old ghost words, the new undead language was first found floating through dictionaries as rare copying errors, reminders that although language clones cleaner than violence or genetics, nothing reproduces   perfectly. But unlike the old ghost words, the new un-words   endured. Unheard of! The unwritten   masterpieces of gutter cleaners, sidewalk snugglers, failed sprinters, abstract chemists, old locals, shamed poets, blind birdwatchers, tweakers, phosphorus gulpers, satirical cartographers, shoplifters, astronomers of despair became subtext which became text which became the new untext.

The language of absence remains untranslatable. But   in the way it haunts our eyes   when we look away some of us have come to understand:

Seventeen Years
by Ann Howells

When he woke frisky this morning,
I thought to cancel.
But bad days outnumber good.
He grows insubstantial,
as though life vaporizes through skin
that hangs like laundry on a line,
and he struggles to rise,
each stiff-legged step painful.

Fur-draped bone
leaves few places to insert a needle.
But he doesn't whimper or struggle.
He trusts me. I feel a turncoat
as I whisper baby-talk: *Sweet Silky Furs*,
Precious Little Man,
Mama's Baby Boy,
till the vet urges me to go.

I am bereft.
My head says *I've spared him pain*,
but my heart cries, *Judas! Betrayer!*
His collar jangles my pocket
as though he still walks with me.

Ghost Mask, Mask Shop, Venice, Italy
by Roger Camp

Two Girls Watching TV
by Valerie Hunter

TV is Ellie's escape
after a long day of work;
she likes slipping into lives
she'll never have, losing herself
in foreign places, giving her heart
to fictional characters.
The British sitcom *Ghosts*
is her favorite because she adores
the ridiculousness and loveliness
of this found family of dead souls.
Of course she knows ghosts aren't real,
but she can't help envying Alison's kinship
with the afterlife. Plus Ben Willbond is hot.

TV is Marcella's escape, too;
a break in the lonely monotony
of her days haunting Ellie's apartment.
She despises *Ghosts*, but
it's not like she gets a say,
and watching anything
is better than watching nothing.
Perhaps she should find the show aspirational;
maybe one day she'll find someone who can
see her, speak to her, befriend her,
but she doubts it. Such powers are nothing more
than a collective mortal hope that the afterlife isn't
the terrible wasteland it actually is.

But when they get to the episode
with the flashback of Robin
the caveman ghost wandering
the grounds of Button House alone,
before Sophie comes along,
Marcella finds herself crying
in recognition,
and when she looks over,
Ellie is tearing up, too,

and for a moment they are just
two girls watching TV together,
engrossed in this world
that's almost theirs.

Excerpts from San Narciso: Republican, Tragic & Romantic novel on Mexican National Affairs
by Joe Galván

Veracruz, Mexico
1937

This morning, I keep my eyes fixed on the sun glitter on the sea. My daughter Juana and her husband Eutímio have just finished visiting me for the second time this year. Her husband is the municipal president of the ward and is also the head of the longshoremen's association. I almost never see him, except for the odd times when he appears for dinner, and even then, he takes his meals in the kitchen with Ignacia. When Juana first married him, he found me funny, as if I were a queer-looking little elf that had stowed away in the trousseau and was only to be summoned when the bedsheets needed folding. He lets me hold court in the patio, watching the warm tropical rain spatter the terracotta tiles. I deliver missives. I give commands. I sometimes say to him, 'Get us some sweet bread from Lara's Bakery by the big church downtown.' I dictate how the house is to be run. Not even my daughter interferes with what I say. I watch the wind rustle the bougainvilleas against the white stucco wall that separates the house from the world and its noise. Just beyond that, the swells sweep over the hot sand of the beach. I hear the clang of bells and bosun's whistles over the din of the restless sea. I sometimes see American warships puff off towards Nicaragua and Honduras and Costa Rica. I see banana boats. I see Mayans, ancient and dark, weave palm fronds into baskets to sell on the street. I see monkeys. I see lime vendors. I see coconut vendors. I smell Spanish verbena and Cuban tobacco and I sometimes hear a band play a *danzón* in the plaza in front of the Cathedral.

    My husband Arturo built this house. It stands, white as a cloud, ringed with blue talavera, at the blue-green lip of the sea. Palm trees frame it. The sun and salt air and the tropical rain scrub the grime from the stucco. Skinks scatter under the fallen fronds. Our house has a toaster and a percolator and a washing machine. Juana can afford to crimp her hair in Marcel waves and her daughters do the same. When they come here during Easter and Christmas, my granddaughters arrive in a big black Packard automobile. They put on rouge and lipstick and Chanel No. 5 from the little boutiques in the capital where they buy their dresses. They put records on the Victrola and dance the foxtrot. My youngest granddaughter has just returned from her honeymoon in Spain with shawls of black lace, *peinetas* of mother-of-pearl, and silk drawers. I can have anything I desire, so long as it is reasonably priced. I can have Ignacia make me rice pudding with vanilla from Papantla. I can make a *capirotada* with French bread if I want. I can buy a Chinese parasol from the knickknacks shop near the docks. I can place an order from the Sears catalog the old American sutler keeps in his hot little kiosk in the center of town. I can have anything I want because we have something called a line of credit. I have bought tiny tea sets, spoons for tasting chocolate, a sick call crucifix, entire plans for a house, and dresses that sell for a dollar.

    In the evening, I sit in a wicker rocking chair on the back porch and listen to the sea batter the jetties. Ignacia turns on the radio. We listen to the new bolero they're singing in the capital. We have our coffee. We watch the moon rise. For thirty years, I have sat in this rocking chair, fanning off the horseflies and wading into the sea of memories my mother still lives in. Every time I turn a corner going up the stairs to my bedroom, I remember our white ship of a house in the Laguna Madre in Texas, our hillock of short grass; our bay horse and our pony who died when I was ten. I see the ghost of my mother in her white cotton dress and her thin navy blue belt of worsted wool, its tiny brass buckle whose dull reflection gleamed in the light of a hurricane lamp and which I still see gleaming in the dark of certain nights. When the midnight rains come at the end of the hot season, I open the jalousies and put out my hand and I feel her sweep past me, in a faint gust sated with the breath of the rain.

This year will mark the fifteenth in which the green parrot we kept in the patio as a pet will not sing. It will be seventh since we buried my sister Guadalupe under a *pirul* tree in the Carmelite convent in Jalapa. It will be two years since the death of Chula, my eldest daughter's golden retriever. Her eldest son—my grandson—will be departing on a steamer this year bound for Yale, where he will study how to maintain oil derricks. It will be ten years since we heard that Lindbergh crossed the Atlantic, ten years since the radio told us Spanish partisans had been exiled to Mexico by Franco, ten years since we got a new refrigerator, ten years since Doña Mercedes, my across-the-street neighbor, was persuaded to live in the Capital by her good-for-nothing son, ten years since our housekeeper Ignacia accidentally broke my Chinese vase while watering the chrysanthemums, ten years since we had a big hurricane.

It will be two years since we got the new Cathedral radio I love so much—my husband used to call it 'the wireless' because that was what the traveling salesman insisted that it was called. It will be a year since my favorite eight o'clock novela, *Amores Perfectos*, ended. It will be seven years since the rest of the world went to hell.

It has been a year since my husband Arturo died. It has been a year and a few days since we buried him in the Municipal Cemetery No. 1 where the graves stand like white bricks left out in the hot morning sun, where the weeds clump together and the trees hang forbiddingly low, where the sound of the surf can be heard, where it is too hot to have lunch. It has been a year since the house he built for me at the edge of the sea no longer bustles with the activity it used to, our teenagers, our chickens, our evening serenades. Ignacia sweeping out the rain with broom made of corn straw, making small talk with the boys who sell watermelons and the man who comes to pick up the spare glass bottles.

It has been six months since my daughter Rosalinda came by to escape the tremendous heat in Guanajuato with my son-in-law Severo, a man who I believe is too ugly for her. Severo has a 1930 Ford Model A that he travels to the backlands to sell insurance policies to farmers who cannot read and ranchers who once buried *Federales* during the *Cristiada*. This year, my youngest granddaughter will marry a blond American boy and finally move to California, where she will teach the fandango to the children of vintners and movie stars.

And it will be twenty years, Mother, since you exhaled the last vivid sigh of your being, closed your eyes, and we crossed your arms. It will be twenty years since we closed your coffin, recited the prayer to the Holy Shroud for the repose of your eternal soul, and made empanadas filled with rice and beans to hand out at your wake. It will be twenty years since we parted with the tiny silver earrings mined in San Luis Potosi, twenty years since we removed your turquoise ring and tossed it into the sea so that you would forever marry yourself to it, like the Venetians did long ago; twenty years since we all wore mourning for four months, when I covered the mirrors of our house so your ghost would not become trapped in them.

How will I tell your story to your great-grandchildren? In this mind that cannot remember very much now, in these eyes that can barely see, in these old bones that creak and feel the *chocolatero* winds that descend across the bay from the north in the winter and shake the palm fronds loose on the promenade, the words cannot rise quickly enough. Only words and images scattered against forty years of my own life and yours, with two centuries between them both. Your beauty lives through me, my sons and daughters, in the eyes of my light-skinned grandchildren who know nothing of you except what I can muster up. How will I evoke the beauty of 1867 in you, of '74, of the effervescence of '85 when we took a trip in the landau to visit Doctor Jimenez, who told me I was of marriageable age? The four o'clocks in Xalapa never looked more enticing.

How horrible it was to see your coffin sinking into the soft, hot earth. I was imprisoned thereafter for months by my grief. It was a beautiful prison of love and memory. I admit I loved enshrining you in my sadness, but the pain was locked in me, under layers of black crepe and silk, behind my cameo brooch, bordered in the thick black borders of the stationery we ordered because everyone had to know you were dead. Men wrote me letters lauding your great beauty—letters I could not then read because I no longer understood English—letters that I could not personally respond to because the language of grief choked out whatever response I could give. Only Arturo could speak for me, and his writing was so terse and brittle we didn't have any visitors for a year.

This year, the grief will rise like a swell breaking upon the shore at low tide: it will barely break and sweep across the flat sandy shore of my life, and then it will recede, and it will take with it whatever memory I had of you. I can barely remember your face now. I do remember your eyes, your hands. But there are other things that are hard to place.

My dear Arturo.

You still come to me. You sit on my bed as you used to, and you smile faintly, and you disappear. I am almost always awake—you only think I am sleeping. Sometimes the waves break hard against the seawall and I can feel the house rumble. I'll go to the window and step out on the balcony, look at the stars reach their height against the deep dark blue of the Gulf sky. I'll turn around and there you are, hands folded. Unlike La Llorona or the Headless Mule, you are beautiful, you cannot and do not wish to harm me. You smile faintly, you fade away, and my heart breaks again. Your memory is brilliant and beautiful. If I press my face into the pillow I can smell the brilliantine you wore and only then am I able to sleep again.

Even when the black brows of hurricanes stood you down, you never flinched. Not once. Calmly, assuredly, you'd tell Ignacia to close the shutters. And although we had plenty of rain, the house was so well built that I never lost a thing, save for a palm tree or two. And afterward—once the storm surge had finally relinquished its grip on the town and the police could discern the dead bodies from the living ones—we had coffee as we usually did. Good God, it was so hot. What business did we have asking Ignacia to make us coffee? I suspect that you learned this trait from the English.

Just the other day I thought of you, standing in the door of the house, with my little market basket in hand. In another time and place, Arturo, we'd go to market together. I'd let you pick out the *panes*, the limes, the pineapples, the tomatoes to make the sopas you loved to slurp loudly. Maybe in Heaven there's a *tianguis* we can stroll in, anonymously, while San Pascual sells us chile verde and the Virgin of Guadalupe offers us garlands of roses, the divine delicacies of life eternal. What were you doing while I was at the market? Did you take telephone calls on the second floor? Did you place orders for the workers on the docks? Or did you long for me, for the curve of my bodice and the ruffle of my taffetas, my ribbons, my white cotton shirtwaists and my worn leather boots? I am sure you did as much as I did for you. I longed for you then as I did now. I am not saying Ignacia is terrible company. It was that, for all my life—even now, in my widowhood—I was madly in love with you. The trait that we all have in this family is that we love the men we love to the point of madness.

The crepe myrtles in my front yard nod in the dying purple twilight and the breeze sweeps along the soft cool tiles where I walk barefoot. I walk under the arches of the patio, waiting for Ignacia to come out with a tea set and her knitting bag. She'll pull the radio from the wall and turn the dial all the way to 8 and we'll wait for the booming voice of the announcer from XEW to finish the evening news. Did you hear that the President of the Republic wants to wean us off of Standard Oil? Did you hear that FDR finally stood up from his wheelchair before a ravished crowd of 100,000? Did you hear that Prime Minister Churchill wants to avoid a war with Germany? Did you hear that the Japanese invaded China? Did you hear that they think the world is going to end in a year or so?

But it wouldn't end here. No. My little rocky spit will break off from Mexico and I'll float through the Gulf until I reach the Western Paradise. If one day the Republic finally collapses, I'll go to the top of my house and fly a white flag and we'll sail, Ignacia and me, to Manhattan. But tonight, like the other Tuesday nights of the last year or so, we will wait by the radio to hear another episode of *El Conde de Monte Cristo*. And because Ignacia can neither read nor write, we will spend the next thirty minutes reviewing what we just listened to, as if we had read the novel by that man Dumás, whom the narrator eulogizes. In that moment, Arturo, you become as clear as the Count himself, clad in black leather and a real red cape—red like the cochineal dye for the vestments for the Virgin of Zapopán. It is like I have you here again, those dainty pince-nez glasses sitting on the fat bridge of your Roman nose, book in hand, taking in the world once again as my husband, to survey the quiet kingdom of plants and waves we once owned. The one thing I will miss is your grave—quiet, unassuming, a whitewashed marble plot topped with gravel and an angel quietly lamenting you, contemplating the black beauty of the letters you bore in this life. I can never stay there for too long, because like the heat, the memory of you is too much for me to endure. Would that we were twenty-seven and still good-looking, waiting for the mariachis to strum the last *tin-tan* from the last waltz in the last hour of our wedding. That is the moment I wish us to exist in.

    Once the twilight fades and the night descends, I will embark again on the night journey toward the endless warm sea, abounding with life and dreams. My boat is small, and I carry nothing in it but myself. I don't need to row out far enough for the current to seize me and pull back into 1886, when I stood on the platform of the train station in Mexico City, with the steam rising off a stilled locomotive. I will see your eyes, green as the jungles of Honduras, green as Chiapas and the Mayan ruins, stare back into me. I will smell the mango juice on your fingers, I will taste it on your lips. And when I have savored that instant for a moment the current will draw me onward towards dawn, where I will meet you as the morning star. The entire seno Mexicano will extend her brown naked arms to me, full of parrots and palm trees and the fort of San Juan de Ulua, and she will say goodbye. All Mexico will say goodbye to me, and all of Texas too; and once I am past the Azores and have drifted into the silent space where the prime meridian the equator meet, I ill see you, and then I will know what I have missed all these years.

Pensioner of the Merchant Marine
by Keith Melton

Toiling amidst the smell of peanut oil and potatoes
A stool to hold our port-of-call
We gather in a longshoreman's bar
To tell our split of history
How it was and will never be again.

And left to a generous demise of muscle and work
Pensions too small and odd jobs
We tell of storms that brought our hearts
The stiffness of fear
Praying Hail Mary, full of grace

Recollections of Nazi U-boats
And merchant flags lost no easy watch.
And remembering their faces, ghostly white --
In the blackness of gloom in some tomb
At the end of an unnumbered street

No ceremony beneath the flag, no camaraderie
On a pauper's wooden stack
'Till the ground bores us stiff
To curdle quietly with our bones.
So this is the bond we make in a juke joint, no dream

But to escape the fear of dying alone
Not in Japan, Russia or Singapore
But riding a barstool in the City of Brotherly Love
The wind at our backs, confessors to the grave
The reach of sailing men to the waves.

Haunt Me Gently
by Nicholas Yandell

(To SH, JR, KB, and anyone else I'm forgetting to thank for continuing to haunt me)

Haunt me gently, as your lifetimes reappear. On my windshield reflection, in sudden trepidation. Thought long gone away, in a shifting mind's state. I won't ask you to leave, and I probably never will, despite how uncomfortable thoughts of you make me feel.

Make yourselves known, and I'll start the same way. Apologize for refusing to acknowledge you. Guilty and clouded with substance, unable to dwell on your absence. Because though you are gone, you still exist so vividly. Appearing in wake and sleep. I struggle with such ambiguity, retreating far too easily.

So, haunt me steadily, as the waning blood red pyre sinks into a pool of sky. Mimicking hues in weary eyes, from too many intrusive thoughts. Making me question why I'm still driving this desolate highway all alone. Bearing the friction of restless souls, irritating my fragile state. Barely holding 10 and 2, just to keep this body safe.

But despite the perils, I'll take the risk. I know why I'm out here once again. This time finally with intention. Cruising the meditative asphalt, with wide-eyed aspirations of finding peace, out here in this vast release.

Yes, haunt me swiftly, while I have no escape. No way to ignore the flickers of pain. Sharp twinges of desert mirages. Heavenly wraiths in the light of the moon. Incomplete portraits, whose admirable attributes, are all that shimmers through. I'm just not ready to accept this version of you.

I'd happily take a blemished vessel, dripping sadness, fear and anger. An authentic moment of any kind, if tacked onto your time, no matter how undesirable it seems. But I know this request is just something of my dreams.

So then, haunt me fiercely; that's what I'll ask of you. Though I know I'm not entitled to anything from your recollection. I'm not even close to the one, whom in your exit lost the most. But I can't help feeling the pounding lack. The what ifs and the unknowns. The indelible mark, that too quickly became a scar, tossing me unceremoniously out of naivety.

As my car windows open irrationally, and I'm blown by a smoky breeze, I'll hold tight your apparitions. Finding enigmatic comfort in their diversion. More time to unwind the complexity of living and the fragility of proceeding.

Now, haunt me forcefully, in these shadows of mountains on sprawling dry country. You ghosts who've never left me, who speak persuasively of your mysteries, passionately in time with a steady beat. To whom I'll finally reveal unburdened honesty, while reliving fictional scenarios with many different endings.

And haunt me clearly, even as you're fading. Leaving me a tumbleweed of loneliness turbulently blowing. Straddling the edge of the great planes of mortality. Where I'll say my goodbyes to you, my best of spirit friends in my passenger seats. Having our last tearful conversations, before you'll inevitably disappear. And I'll finally stop moving and this sacred pilgrimage of consolation, will blur into the trickling warmth of memory.

So please, just haunt me gently, through these last rumbles. The passing aggressions of nature's expression, amplified in my digressions. Where I'm so thankful for your persistence. The chance to ponder your resting souls, with these extra ticks of existence. An epilogue for tender growth, to examine all our lives exposed, while out here navigating so many unknowns, all along the dusty road on my survivor's journey.

Ancestors
by Lynette Esposito

She had ghosts in her blood--
born with them in her cells--
raised with them--
heard their voices at night
when her mother said prayers.

When her babies were born,
the ghosts followed the children
to their new lives –
born in their cells.
Ghosts knew them
from their mother's
nightly prayers
when she spoke their names.

Granny's Ghost
by Sarah Das Gupta

I see her now, raking the fire
with an old brass poker,
sparks fly up in protest
at such brazen intrusion
into their warm,
drowsy dying.

She is afraid of death,
avoids any tv murder,
or prolonged, fatal illness.
Drawn out, death bed dramas,
occasions to put the kettle on,
to rake the fire to ashes,
to put the cat out, again.

In the end she went suddenly,
Feeling dizzy, took two aspirin.
Sat down for ten minutes.
Didn't get up again.

No one rakes the fire now-
it's all gas and electric.

What Cannot Be Changed
by KB Ballentine

Even with Samhain closing in,
   there's no fog or mist
that divides the living and the dead.
   I'm already a ghost –
a brief blur you might remember.
   No halo around the hunter's moon
where clouds hover then shrug
   and move on. Maples and oaks shuffle
what's left of their leathered leaves,
   bear the crow as he balances
between midnight and morning.

Out There
by S.Z. James

    We moved out there in spring. The trees in that place were something to see, out in the wind, blowing like nothing all day and night, howling through the cracks. The lights were small, and our faces loomed big at each other all night around that little table. I set to work. There were ditches to be dug, holes to be filled in. We didn't find anything out in the woods until later, but when we did I decided to do something about it. It felt good, that summer and into the fall, watching the waves whiten and collapse down the slope, and drinking that tea made from the lavender we found growing in the grasses out there. I finally managed to get some decent work done, not being in that little place anymore, with all that noise. Out here was silence, the real kind, that you only dream about when you live in one of those boxes, and it was the thing for work. Sometimes we would walk down the slope and look at the seagulls picking at a dead seal or find some kelp or a jellyfish washed up and poke at it, talk about the smell. Other times we would walk in the woods, hear the wind in the boughs and talk about the sun, or the earth, or not talk at all, just walk and listen and be out there. It turned up one afternoon, right as the sun was turning its way down to the salt. We were on the porch, I don't remember what else. It came out of the woods. I thought it was a deer. We'd seen a few of those around. Once we even saw a bear, a little one, and it looked sad and we sort of felt sorry for it, but it ran off. But it wasn't a deer. I don't know. It was something else. It might have been a big cat, maybe. It was sleek like one, anyway, and moved like one, but it didn't look like a cat, or a dog, or an animal, really, it was just itself, which was fine, since that's all you can really ask of anything. Like I said I decided to do something about it. I got off the porch and waved my arms at it to try and make it get out of there, and it did. We didn't mean to be mean to it or anything like that, it's just what you do. It came back later, I think a week later, and I was in the kitchen doing something and saw it out the window, over the flower bed and the railing of the porch. I thought of the last time, and how I'd been sorry. So I didn't swing my arms at it again, didn't do anything really, just watched it. Followed it with my eyes around the yard, for a while. It just moped around. After a while it climbed a tree, and I stopped watching and did something else, and when I looked again it was gone. Later I was out in the woods and I found what must have been its nest, or its home. There wasn't much, some sticks, a piece of garbage that must have been from the beach. It was sort of sad, looking that way, and I decided to do something about it. I went back to the house and got some wood from the woodpile and brought it back and built the nest up into a little lean-to, against a tree. I want to think it liked that, but it was hard to tell. I never went near there again. The next time I saw it we were out there on the beach, and it was there in the waves, ducking under them like it was looking for something it had lost down there. We just kept walking and left it alone. It was a whole year before we saw it again. We decided it had migrated. Then I saw it for just a second ducking behind the woodpile, or what I thought was it. I looked around but couldn't find it anywhere. One day we found a pile of fish on the porch, which was nice, not having to catch them ourselves. The fish kept turning up, but we didn't see it anywhere anymore. We thought it was repaying our kindness for building the lean-to. I guess we saved it the trouble of building a new one. But then the bad part happened. I wish it hadn't, and it wasn't anyone's fault, of course, but it did, and there you go. One night we're in bed, late, the moon is out and full coming through the curtain. I get up to go to the bathroom, and come back to find there it is, standing in the bedroom. Naturally I make a big noise, and then the lights are on and it doesn't want to be in here anymore and makes a break for it. Heads for the door. Goes right through me! I swear, I've never felt anything like that. It felt like sticking your finger in pudding, but inside out, where the pudding is sticking its finger in you. Best way to explain it, I've tried everything. After that we moved. I felt bad for scaring it like that, but if it was going to start coming into our bedroom uninvited, that's what's going to happen. So we packed up all our things, and said goodbye to the place, and the trees, and the wind, and the salt down there and that wonderful silence. Haven't been back since. I've wanted to a few times, just so we know it's still there, but I'm worried if we do we might not leave again. It really is something to see out there. It's like heaven on earth, to me, anyway.

I Summon Our Dead Sister to Our Dying Father's Bedside

by Gabby Gilliam

You enter the room
the mirror of our mother
chestnut curls and beryl eyes.

You perch on the edge of the bed
so carefully it doesn't shift beneath
your weight—an impossible ghost
here to hold my hand
when I need comfort most.

I ask how you found us—our other sisters
settled on the opposite side of the bed
attention focused on our father
delirious and gasping between our worry
his skin purpling with the bruise of death.

You squeeze my hand
and say you followed
the furrow of our grief.

THE FAMILY GHOST
by Dee Allen

I was summoned from the void by a witch named Suzanne
Who named me, faced execution in her village in Scotland.
Her daughter Deborah was spared, taken to safety in Holland,
Her own power grew under the watch of a Talamasca man,
Whom she, as an adult, came to seduce—
A numinous legacy bound to be produced—
Then came Charlotte, favourite mine,
Left Holland for the Caribbean, continued the bloodline.
Then Jeanne-Louise inherited the land & wealth, family claim.
Despite marriage, she held on to the family name.
Then came Angelique—a female twin.
Then Marie-Claudette moved her family from the Caribbean.
Then came Katherine—the weaker one.
Julian—her brother—the warlock son.
I was Mary Beth's punishing strong arm.
Stella—the fun lover, the first to reject my charm.
Carlotta—the cruel, blinded Antha so she couldn't see
Because Antha—from girlhood—was loyal to me.
Carlotta's next victim—poor Deidre—"Incapable", her status
Had baby and estate taken from her, drugged, driven to madness.
What that hag called "protecting them from me"!
I aided their family for centuries! Didn't she see?
And lastly came Rowan—thirteenth in line.
Only she could end this loneliness of mine.
Everything achieved by this arcane clan went according to my plan.
One wish needs fulfilling: I want to be a man,
Roam around in your physical reality.
A union with my dearest heart—Rowan's the key.
That boundless obsession, driving me the most,
Would be a welcome change from my current state—"The Family Ghost".

Through incestuous matings and marriages, the family grew
On plantations and estates between New Orleans and Saint Domingue.
Everybody felt envy and fear of this clan of witches,

Powerful in the supernatural and their riches.
They owe it all to me—their watcher, their protector—
Written off by some as an interfering brown-haired spectre.

I am deeply connected to the Mayfairs.
Bound to the young female heirs
Through the emerald necklace each wear—
Speak my name and rest assured, I'll be there.
I am your servant, reliable swift hand.
Name your desire, dear. Lasher awaits your command.

Talamasca: A secret society of psychic detectives.

Tricks Mix
by Ken Gosse

I once met the Ghost of Lim Rix.
Named Anon, he used mischievous tricks
to taunt and persuade me
and finally made me
rhyme words which we never should mix.

Sabrina
by Christine Eskilson

Shortly after losing my best friend, I met Alan and his daughter, Sabrina, at a local support group. Over the years I lived through Lori's biopsy, diagnosis, chemotherapy, radiation, remission, reoccurrence, and then her agonizingly slow death as she fruitlessly sought more trials and more treatments. Alan and Sabrina's loss was much more abrupt. A man behind the wheel after too many hours in front of the bar took a wife and mother in a head-on collision. He escaped with bruises and a broken collarbone. She died in an ambulance.

I warmed to Alan's kind open face right away. Sabrina was another story. Her closely set blue eyes never seemed to blink beneath short, blunt bangs, and her square jaw and snub nose made for an unusually ugly child.

I'd been attending the weekly group at the community center for a few months when one evening, as our meeting broke up, Alan invited me to dinner. Or rather he asked Sabrina, who hovered behind him, if she would mind if I joined them. Sabrina shrugged, which Alan took as a yes and turned to me inquiringly.

"I'd be happy to," I said. I tried a big smile at Sabrina but she'd taken a sudden interest in the scuffed floor tiles.

Over pasta at a nearby Italian restaurant Sabrina stared at me from underneath those awful bangs. Alan had excused himself for an urgent business call, leaving an awkward silence. We'd already run through the usual topics; Sabrina was almost thirteen, her favorite school subject was history, and on the weekends she enjoyed picking the wings off flies. No, that last one was my own mean-spirited addition. When I asked about hobbies, she simply shrugged again.

Sabrina broke the quiet by clattering her fork on her plate. "Do you believe in ghosts?"

"Uh, no," I replied, taken aback. "Do you?"

She leaned forward over her buttered penne, her voice lowering to a whisper. "Yes. My mom promised me she'd never leave me and she didn't. She leaves me notes on my bathroom mirror."

"Does your dad know about this?"

"I showed him once but he got really sad. Now I just wipe them off after I read them."

Alternating between pity and feeling slightly unnerved by the girl, I took an easy way out and repeated a platitude from our support group. "Our loved ones will always be with us."

Sabrina drew back in her chair and fixed me with a scornful look. Over her right shoulder Alan approached our table. "Sorry about that. Ready to go, ladies?"

Her face cleared and she smiled up at him. "Ready to go, Dad."

I married Alan six months later. The like at first sight had matured into love and I felt ready to be a wife for the first time. And a mother figure, too, I supposed, although I didn't dwell on that. I'd asked Sabrina to be my junior attendant but on the day of the wedding she claimed a nasty cold and refused to leave her room. After an all too brief honeymoon while Sabrina stayed with a distant cousin, I sold my condo and moved across town into their sprawling home.

Although Alan assured me I could do what I liked with the house, I hesitated to make changes. I didn't know what Sabrina was contemplating behind those unblinking eyes and I didn't want to disturb our fragile co-existence. In the end I took the modest step of replacing the austere pale gray walls of our master bedroom and bath with a cheerful butter yellow.

Alan said he loved the new color. Sabrina didn't say anything. For the next week she wore only gray sweats.

One morning a message greeted me on my bathroom

mirror. Neatly printed in blue marker read the words: *Please Don't Forget Me.* I snatched up a washcloth to wipe away the letters. Sabrina, I thought. What kind of game was she playing?

Alan was away on a business trip so I took matters into my own hands and stalked into her room. "Did you write on the mirror?"

Sabrina looked up from her book with interest. "It must be your friend, Lori. What did she say?"

I shook my head. "Don't lie to me. Just don't do it again."

But she did. The same message appeared on the mirror over the next few weeks. Each time I scrubbed it away. I didn't complain to Alan; this was between me and Sabrina. Instead I devised a plan to persuade him to get her out of the house.

"Boarding school?" she asked skeptically when we told her.

Alan nodded. "Mom went there. She loved it. Obviously it's a little far just to pop home for dinner but you'd be here on holiday breaks and even on some weekends if you'd like."

Those weekends would be few and far between, I silently vowed.

After some consideration Sabrina agreed to go. Alan took her to the school to get her situated while I enjoyed the luxury of a childless home and a clean bathroom mirror.

When the distraught phone calls began I urged Alan to ignore them. "It's an adjustment, sweetheart. She's going to be fine." The school agreed with my advice even as they escalated. Then, one evening, silence.

Alan answered when the school head called the next morning. I had to pry the phone from his fingers as he moaned, "No, I don't believe it. It can't be."

Sabrina was dead. She'd climbed to the top of the clock tower on campus and flung herself a hundred feet to a brick walkway below.

I tried to comfort Alan but he could barely look at me. It's not my fault, I wanted to scream. I left him sobbing in the kitchen and retreated to our bedroom suite.

A fresh message, this time scrawled in black marker, awaited on my bathroom mirror: *You Will Never Forget Me.*

Those Whose Memories I Share
by Ann Howells

In these waters lie graves
of my father's blood, ancestors
whose final breath was water –
rows of savage mountains,
mantle of sea closing around them.

They understood wind change,
barometric drops, electric smell of lightning.
Tide seeped inside their shells,
turned in their bones – nowhere to hide.

A glass dome covers me,
covers ruffled bay, whispering pines,
this old house –
a second heart holding memories
and familiar ghosts.

Waves fling themselves upon shore,
battle flags flying,
in ceaseless effort to reclaim land.
The pier, marimba of warped boards,
plays a funeral song.

Rata Udre Udre
by Mike Wilson

     I
(in *i Takei*, a/k/a Fiji, *circa* 1840)

Drumming thrumming through thick forest trees
makes hearts race – the *i Takei* freeze,
listening to the *lali*, wooden drum
telling what has passed or what's to come.

Do *i uauas* beat a celebration
sounding boisterous congratulations
to a mother nursing her newborn?
Is the *lali*'s resonance forlorn

tidings of an uncle who has died?
No, this *lali* warns that war betides,
time to follow our ferocious Rata,
seizing in our huts our favorite *gata*

clubs of *vesi* wood that make men moan
when the angled edges snap their bones,
clubs inlaid with teeth of enemies
killed and eaten in our victories.

Cowards scurry to a hiding place
hoping blood's sweet copper scent's not traced
by a hungry nose as *gatas* raise
raining blows and knocking foes sideways.

From old Korolevu comes the sound
heard in Dakudaku hills around:
Rata Udre Udre, greatest chief,
stealing life and joy from others' grief.

Hear the *lali*'s gruesome lullaby?
Be a man, prepare yourself to die!
Rata Udre Udre's *lali* beats!
Rata Udre Udre wants to eat!

II

After battle, we will have a snack -
noses sliced and roasted from the stack
of bodies piled that we will need to gut,
then in parts for packing off, we'll cut

into segments at the joints, then braise
blocking rotting as we wend our way
back to Korolevu, on the hill
where we'll feast, in sanctity, our fill.

Every man will eat from one he slayed
but the prisoner booty will be saved
for our Rata, his to eat alone,
marking each one with a massive stone

lined beside the others, giant beads
of an abacus recording deeds,
swallowed lives, an awe-inspiring sight,
monument to Rata's appetite.

When we near the rock walls of our fort,
then begin the songs of our consorts
and excited children dance and cheer
father-warriors, who have twice killed fear;

once, the fear of foes that we have slaughtered;
twice, the harbored fears of sons and daughters
for whom we bring *bokola* for meat
so that relatives we need not eat.

Eat we must, but not ourselves to please –
we kill for the god we must appease
as directed by the bete priests;
if the god is happy, we can feast.

III

Scouting from our village hilltop, high,
no one comes to rescue, none will try.
Sea surrounding also we can view –
only waves, no saviors in canoes.

Joyous, we march booty from the raid,
beaten bloody, into the stockade.
Men and women with their children weep,
clutch in vain the life they cannot keep.

So much *bokola* we killed won't fit
Korolevu's *lovo* oven pits.
So, we make the prisoners dig another
where we'll roast their fathers and their mothers.

When they finish digging and are tired,
they are made to gather for the fire
kindling sticks and branches that aren't green
so the *lovo* oven pit burns clean.

We unpack our sacks of captured lives,
handing pieces out along with knives
dressing flesh while bete supervise
cutting up of *bokola* to size.

Prisoners watch as we prepare their kin,
elders, fathers, brothers, sons, and friends,
hang their virile parts in sacred trees,
balls and penis dangling in the breeze.

We scorch body pieces to prepare
for removal of the skin and hair
scraping with the *kai*, or bi-valve shells.
As we work, we feel our hunger swell.

IV

Bokola we wrap inside *tudano*,
malawaci, *yudi* or in *dalo*
leaves, like little sleeves for baking flesh,
rolled with garden vegetables dug fresh.

But before we start to cook the meat,
Rata Udre Udre takes his seat:
"Prisoners, you must honor me, the chief.
 Make a cup from this banana leaf."

With his bamboo knife he cuts their vein,
holds their cup below it as it drains,
vibrant redness pouring in a flood,
and they watch great Rata drink their blood.

Flesh must be baked slowly, so to render
chunks of tough and stringy meat to tender
morsels, but our hunger agitates;
doing useful work will help us wait.

We will smash the mouths of severed heads
of *bokola* to harvest from these dead
teeth to inlay in their killers' *gatas*,
giving holy warrior power, *mana*,

or to string in necklaces to wear
with *tobe*, rings of our *bokolas*' hair,
woven in a lanyard showing stature.
Long bones, split, we'll carve into back-scratchers.

Sau-ni-laca, needles that can sew
sails for ships, we'll make from their shin bones.
Even empty skulls will have a use -
bowls from which we'll drink *yaqona* juice.

V

In the temple, by the *lovo* pits
where the roaring fire flames and spits,
bete intone prayers to make the meat
that we offer to the god taste sweet.

In a pot some fruit and flesh we toss,
stewing up a toothsome special sauce
stirred with spoons made of *bokola* bones,
smelling so piquant, *i Takei* moan.

Nose-delighting carnival, so carnal,
simmering in ovens of the charnel
lovo makes us hunger-maddened, weeping.
and the Rata Udre Udre, leaping

to his feet with wild eyes, lifts his hand,
points it jailward, shouts out his command:
"Bring that prisoner quickly to my seat!
Rata Udre Udre wants to eat!"

Warriors throw the man at Rata's feet.
"Raise him up and hold him still to meet
fate I have conceived; pry wide his jaw,
take this hook, then reach inside his maw.

"Pierce his tongue and stretch it like a snake.
Take a knife and cut it off to slake
hunger till my feast is finally served
and I'll give him honor he deserves."

Turning to the prisoner, Rata said,
"If you stand tall, disregarding dread,
when I roast your tongue, I'll cut in two;
your own roasted tongue I'll share with you!"

VI

Savory smells surround us, flavory shroud.
Hungry, watery mouths begin to crowd
lovo oven pits, where women ferry
cooked *bokola* from the fire and carry

tender pieces to the chiefs and priests,
after which we all begin to feast!
Free or slave, all sitting in our places;
human grease runs down our happy faces!

Pig is good, but people taste the best -
such is what the gods eat. We are blessed
when *bokola* stuffs our bulging cheeks.
While we dine, our hero chieftain speaks:

"I am Udre Udre, highest Rata!
I have the most *mana* in my *gata*.
I mark all my meals with giant stones
counting all the spirits that I own.

With one more, I will become a god!"
Immortality? We all were awed.
That is why we did not hear or see
an Englishman approaching quietly.

But Rata saw him and said "Who are you
who comes to Korolevu to intrude
upon our sacred feasting? Pink-faced liar,
speak before we roast you in the fire!"

The man said, "I am here for Jesus, who
gave his blood and body up for you."
Rata smiled and said, "That is good news.
Come to the killing stone, and you can, too!"

VII
(in *i Takei*, a/k/a Fiji, 2018)

I flew in from Wellington to Fiji.
This was recommended as a 'must-see' -
some stone tomb belonging to a cannibal.
A lady asked, "Was this guy like a 'Hannibal'?"

The native guide smiled – he'd heard that before.
"Like Hannibal, but Udre kept a score.
See those stones? Eight-hundred-ninety-two.
And some are missing. Udre wasn't through

till he ate nine-hundred-ninety-nine.
With just one more, he could have been divine."
"You mean a god?" she asked. "Like Jesus, really?"
"That's the legend," he said. "Probably silly."

Something stuck inside, like memory,
made this place seem like a rectory.
"How'd he die?" I asked. The guide's smile froze.
"Some say he was shot, but no one knows."

Others left, and underneath the tree
sheltering Udre's tomb was only me.
I heard drumming from a distant shore;
my guide whispered, "Udre ate one more.

"Now he's living in the astral plane
where he beats his *lali*, but in vain.
In that world there is no flesh to roast;
he will always be a hungry ghost."

Soft, I heard a gruesome lullaby. . .
I've become a god that cannot die.
Rata Udre Udre's lali beats!
Rata Udre Udre wants to eat!

Early March
by Lynette Esposito

When spring comes,

frost ghosts

new grass blades--

flowers hold their breath

shiver--waiting

until the chill has passed.

Then open their blooms

beneath the warm sun

unafraid.

Tenth Muse; or, Callisto of Lesbos
by Ivy Jong

They come to me for a summer, saying, oh Sappho, teach me song and poetry and all things lovely which trickle like honey off the tongue.

Here, in fields a-hum with bees and studded with clover, away from the eyes of men, they sit in circles and learn meter and cadence and turn of phrase.

I learn of all the things I cannot have.

Fevered flushes on milky cheeks, peach-down on arms and sunburnt legs sprawled in the grass, freckles scattered across shoulders, white scars on sun-browned skin, thin baby hairs at the napes of necks, translucent crescent moons of fingernails, rosy fingers plucking lyre strings, mouths stained red with the juice of strawberries, pudge of soft fat around the stomach, sweet smell of powder mixed with sweat in the sun, the suggestion of firm roundness beneath the folds of a peplos.

Violets laid in their laps which their fingers weave into crowns as they recite.

Skirts laden with apples and pomegranates, lifted above thin knobby ankles, bare feet in their dusting of earth, white and brown arms reaching in high arcs above their heads to snatch their prizes from the branches.

They are *nymphê*, teetering between girl and woman, between daughter and wife. When they leave they will be ready for marriage. But not yet.

For a season, they belong not to their fathers or their husbands, but with me. For a moment, they are mine.

There is no time in their lives when they belong to themselves.

Callisto loved a woman once. It was her goddess, Artemis, whose fleet footsteps she followed after, racing through the woods and over the hills in their pack of virgin girls. Deer-shooter huntresses, bare-footed, wild-hearted, running feral and free as long as the sun hung in the sky. At night she dreamed of her goddess's white arms encircling her in their embrace. But her fresh face caught the eye of Zeus, who took her in the guise of her beloved, while she laughed with the joy of a love thought hopeless, finally requited.

When dawn's pale light rose on her lying flush and bare in the grass, the one she loved most turned away from her. *No longer virgin*, Artemis accused her. *No longer maiden. No longer mine.*

Cruel goddess, hard as silver, cold as moonlight. As changing in your affections as the phases of the moon in the dark sky.

All maidens follow your example. They swear to me they are mine. In the night they come to me and we hold one another in soft arms, and they claim they are my maiden of the moon. But in the harsh light of day where they may be seen by prying eyes, they grow distant, and in a season they are a blushing bride, thanking me for all I have done for them, pressing my hand in theirs and letting it slip away.

I sing their wedding songs. I praise their good fortune in receiving Aphrodite's blessing–I who have begged for it in tears each night and woken to an empty place beside me–and pretend that I shed tears of joy.

I play their Callisto, fool for believing in their words of loyalty, for worshiping at their feet.

I believe the next will be the one who does not leave me.

Bitter-sweet Eirana,
Fickle Atthis,
Anactoria who swore she did not want to go, that it broke

her to part, who has not sent one word for me.

I am sick to death of the sound of goodbyes.

The deep tone of the barbitos' strings strikes resonant with my heart. They say it suits me more than the light-hearted lyre, that I have always been best at tragedies, and I can only laugh.

So often have we laughed together at the expense of the male sex. I say men are tyrannical, oafish, rough. True, they agree. True, so true dear Sapph, true my love, all too true. Then why leave? Why go to them on your wedding day, giddy, crowned in flowers, draped in saffron and veiled in joy? Have you loved me so little that you cannot even feign regret? Why does the coldest treachery always come from the sun that once filled my life with the warmest of light? Why is it always the hand which I held most dear and beloved in all the world, which always wields and twists the knife? Dear Gods, why shape me from the clay and set desire in my heart for all the things I cannot grasp?

I have grown tired of being the plaything of cruel girls and crueler gods.

I have swallowed an obol to pay the ferryman; I long to see him. I have fastened anklets of stones around my feet. The rope chafes my skin, but I do not feel the burn. The salt in the air, the cries of the gulls, the crash of the waves against the cliffs greet me home.

Say farewell to your dear Callisto. May the waters of the Lethe work quick. When their brackish taste bathes my tongue and stings my throat, may all my memories be erased like our footsteps in the sand by ocean waves, where we once walked side by side. May I forget every soul I ever loved, who left me to drown alone.

Proper ID Required
by Karla Linn Merrifield

As I was sorting it all out,
I found among my brother's papers
his passport application, completed.
And official photos shot
a year before he died.
He must have been two pinched to file.

Whereas I am flush, I realize,
thus properly documented.
Border crossings, customs, proof
of citizenry? No problem.

Just this summer
on my first trip north
I crossed the border via Lewiston-Queenston,
heading to Lake Erie's Pelee National Park.
I returned across the border,
same bridge to stateside,
then west to Niagara Falls,
Niagara County, New York.

Next week I'll cross the border
on the Thousand Island Bridge
into Ontario, Canada, again.
Week after that, I'll return across the border
out of Kingston, ferry to Wolfe Island,
from there ferry to Cape Vincent, USA.

This summer I travel lighter.
His ghost can't cross
the borderline to life.

Merlin Merlot
by A.A. Slaterpryce

Lips stained blue from the holy, splashed ichor,
& in your eyes lies something, an ember, a shine—
a wicked, sick rendition of the barest fire's flicker.

She stands among fires & piles of ash, sicker
than her deceased, stomach like a brine,
lips stained blue from the holy, splashed ichor.

You laugh. She chokes on a sob. You sni—
& cough on acrid clouds of smoke; a foul wine,
a wicked, sick rendition of the barest fire's flicker.

Skeletal fingers pull her up, your heart beats quicker.
Who placed her in a fountain? She drinks, lost in time,
lips stained blue from the holy, splashed ichor.

Cold seeps in, wit sharp, as if to finally trick her.
But you think, "No, she will always be mine."
A wicked, sick rendition of the barest fire's flicker,

burns & singes your hopes, so you turn to liquor.
She is a frozen smile, hot ice growing from her spine,
lips stained blue from the holy, splashed ichor:
a wicked, sick rendition of the barest fire's flicker.

GHOST

SOPHIA SPISAK

TO MEET A GHOST IS QUITE AN HONOR

THEY LIKE YOU ENOUGH TO VISIT

ALL THE WAY FROM THE DEAD.

The Exorcism
by Kara McMullen

Of course it was nearly dark, of course the music stopped abruptly so that the only sound was the pop-and-tick of tires over the gravel driveway, of course the headlights picked up and threw uncanny shadows against the house as Jim and Mona pulled up in the moving truck. They sat in the cab without talking, the truck not even in park yet, looking at their new house, taking in its molting grey shingles, its wickedly sloped veranda, its turret with boarded windows on the northeast corner. A ring of maples surrounded the roof like guards, spiky leaves flushed red in their last, grasping days.

Stirring to life, Mona hopped out before Jim even unbuckled. She lit the last of a joint she'd been nursing all day, and then she was at the house, key in one hand and joint in the other, couldn't even remember fighting across the lawn through the thick deep honey-colored grass, with Jim shouting something at her back—"Hey, wait for me!"— that she ignored. The key stuck in the lock, and the front door only opened after she applied all her weight. Inside it was dark but when her eyes adjusted she saw that the living room was oak paneled, with a pressed tin ceiling and a fireplace large enough to roast a vast army of chickens. Deep scratches in the floor of the foyer seemed to spell something out, although in no language she understood. She took a deep drag as she walked across the dim room, accompanied by the sound of creaking floorboards (of course the floorboards creaked) and dropped the end of the joint in the fireplace.

The house was old and tumbledown, two states to the north, and as far from an interstate as it was possible to get, but Mona and Jim had bought it anyway. Until that day they'd only seen pictures on the real estate website where Mona found it: awkward angles that highlighted pestilential stains on the carpet and walls that were indecent with mold. Even still, the house seemed to offer something that Mona wanted to take—

and Mona was getting good at taking what she wanted. She wanted it because she'd spent all the gruesomely hot days of that summer working from home on the bed in their non-air-conditioned studio apartment. She wanted it because the bar scene was getting old and because her plan to be a painter, to display her art in pristine settings full of rich people nodding obsequiously, had not yet materialized, and in fact showed no signs of doing so in any future she could reasonably imagine. On top of all that, things with Jim would be better with more space and aside from its faults the house was big, three stories plus an attic. Mortgage payments were half what the rent was on the studio, and that was how she finally talked Jim into it. Jim never could turn down a good deal.

When she went back outside Jim was standing near the truck and stretching, lacing his fingers together and raising his arms over his head. His back cracked, and Mona laughed and called him an old man as she reached up to ruffle his hair. Together they watched the sun crawl below the hunched backs of the hills and the sky turn pink and apricot—colors too earnest to use in a painting but that in nature Mona forgave. A crow flew close enough that she felt the breeze from its wings before it swooped up and landed with a croak on the roof of the house.

"Does the electricity work?" Jim asked, looking at the crow.

"I…I don't know, I didn't even check." It hadn't occurred to her that something as fundamental as electricity might not work, and now she had a stricken look on her face. Jim laughed at the stricken look and grabbed a box to bring inside.

The house, of course, was haunted. During a beer break, under the emaciated yellow light of the only fixture in the kitchen (the electricity did work, although fitfully, like a sleeping infant), the ghost of a woman appeared before them. There was a long moment of silence, and then Mona numbly dropped her Miller High Life. As a wave of foamy liquid spread across the cracked linoleum, the ghost introduced herself. Her name was Heidi. She talked for some time, explaining her death (officially, a mix-up with a dosage of laudanum) and her situation (the unholy physics that presided over such things forced her to remain, always, in the house). She gesticulated with long pale fingers as she spoke.

To Mona, Heidi looked more like a sommelier at an innovative restaurant—someone who would tell you that a wine tasted like running through a field with your mouth open—than a ghost. Her hair was cut in a french bob, and she wore a linen smock, the kind of woman who had she lived now would have eventually transitioned to an entirely Eileen Fisher based wardrobe. It was a specific look, but slightly more bourgeoisie than what Mona would have expected from a ghost. Mona stirred to life and mopped up the spilled beer, wondering if her joint had been laced with hallucinogens.

"So you've been here, how long?" Jim asked. He was adjusting quickly. Mona struggled to open another bottle.

"Far too long," Heidi said. "You can't imagine the years. Hundreds of years, more or less. It would have driven me crazy without my practice."

Jim thought about it for a second and then said, "Oh, you're an artist?" He pushed his hair out of his eyes and looked at Mona. "She is too. Or was, maybe? Trying to be? What do you think, babe? How would you describe it?" Mona smiled thinly but did not answer.

"What's your medium?" Heidi asked.

"Um, painting?"

"What mode do you work in?"

"A little bit like Cindy Sherman does the Dutch masters," Mona said, almost automatically. It was the way she'd described her work when she'd applied to grad school and thank god she'd been rejected everywhere because at least she'd never been forced to actually paint whatever that meant. "But like Jim said, I haven't figured it out yet."

"Well try dying. That'll give you time to figure a lot of things out," Heidi said and coughed out a sound that must have been a laugh. After a beat Jim laughed too.

"What can you do?" Jim asked.

"What do you mean?" Heidi said.

"I mean, ghosts can, like, walk through walls and stuff?"

Almost before he finished speaking, the kitchen went dark, and then they watched as Heidi grew as pale and moist as the belly of a fish. A black vein appeared on her forehead and tarry blood vessels were now visible on her cheeks, as though her skin was turning increasingly opaque in an effort to exhibit whatever wretched matter lived inside of her. A dark line in her forehead pulsed and, a sickening second later, broke the surface of her skin. The vein paused, vibrating slightly in the cool air, then detached itself with a wiggling motion. Freed from its bondage, it wormed its way to her scalp, where it disappeared amongst the hair that had, somehow, become a writhing mass.

The next moment the light came back on and Heidi was as before, tired looking and strange and kind of chic. "Does that count?" she asked.

"Good enough for me," Jim said. "Oh, and that reminds me, babe," he continued, turning to Mona, "we've gotta set up the WiFi so we can work tomorrow."

Over lukewarm cups of instant coffee on their second morning, they decided that a ghost for a roommate was something they could live with. More importantly, they decided that Mona would quit her temp job. It was Mona's idea but Jim came around in the end. It didn't pay enough anyway, the mortgage was cheap enough already, and that way she could work on the house, or coordinate the work on the house when it was beyond her abilities. Most of it was beyond her abilities, Mona thought but didn't say. The foundation was crumbling, floors were slanted, and a mushroom colony was moistly thriving in the cave-like room that had once been the butler's pantry. The grayish, shedding paint that covered everything, inside and out, was almost certainly lead-filled and the chimney listed this way and that in high winds. Still, that afternoon Mona opened a beer and gamely fell to tearing up the stained carpet, which exhaled brown cotton balls of dust as she worked. Over the next few days, she set up a composting toilet and removed sections of crumbling drywall and pulled rotten wainscoting off the walls and set out humane rat traps. When she'd caught enough of the creatures she donned yellow latex gloves and a mask and gingerly drove a county over to release them in stubbled gray fields, watching as they blinked and scurried.

Soon the house was less livable than when they'd moved in. Jim barricaded himself in the one viable room downstairs—it had fleur-de-lis wallpaper that Mona was itching to scrape off—and worked on his endless spreadsheets. Heidi, meanwhile, spent her time in the attic making her art. She called them her Mix-Ups and the attic was full of them, things like flattened basketballs attached to antique egg beaters and threadbare stuffed animals sprouting water bottles where appendages should be. Heidi's favorite Mix-Up was one that resembled a hunched vulture in shape and size but was constructed of a broken flowerpot, a deflated pillow, an ancient flip-flop and several tennis balls cut in half. Everything was mounted together to create a gravity-defying, knee-high goblin-like creature that seemed needy to Mona in some oblique way.

Heidi had also commandeered a room in the turret for a painting studio and talked Mona into providing the canvas and the paints. The world in which Mona thought of herself as a painter was further away than ever, so she shrugged as Heidi began setting up easels. With Jim and Heidi busy, Mona focused on other things. Some days she devoted herself virtuously to the house, scraping her knees against the rough wood as she pulled up mangled trim or coughing as she removed an ancient and defunct wasps' nest from the hall closet. Other days she scrolled on the internet for hours, watching videos with millions of views where people rated cookies according to how much they resembled Tom Cruise. Sometimes she read interviews with artists (sparingly because it was an activity that made her feel vertiginous, as though she was looking down from a great height). Mona had begun thinking she would explore performance art, although she was not sure, yet, what the performance would be. It might take some time to find, but she was certain there was something inside her worth excavating.

After a few weeks of this routine, Mona convinced Jim they were ready for a housewarming party. The wires that hung from bare studs and the fact that there was still a bucket instead of pipes under the kitchen sink were actually a positive thing, she explained—it meant they could have a real old-fashioned rager. Jim agreed (Jim always agreed) and once that decision was made they had hushed discussions about Heidi, torn between offending her and scaring their friends. In the end, on the morning before the party, Jim asked Heidi if she wouldn't mind not telling anyone she was a ghost. With a little blush, her pallor could be addressed.

"Are you embarrassed by me?" Heidi asked mildly. Mona and Heidi were sitting on stools around the improvised kitchen table that had sawhorses for legs while Jim dried the breakfast dishes.

"No, it's not that we're embarrassed," Mona said as she picked through a bowl of nuts, looking for the cashews. "It's just that it might freak people out."

"Maybe it could be fun to pretend to be alive for a night?" Jim asked over the banging of the dishes as he put them away. Jim never did anything quietly.

Heidi shrugged. "Maybe when I first died. But the entire concept of living is simply not interesting to me anymore."

"It's just for the party," Mona urged. "This way you can talk to people about your art. If they knew you were a ghost that's all they'd want to talk about."

"Fine, I'll do it," said Heidi, with the air of someone making a great concession.

The night of the party people filled the shell of the house and then spilled outside, where there was a grill full of meat and a portable speaker devoted to a playlist Mona had spent hours curating. Mona found that after spending so much time in her own orbit the gravity of others was destabilizing. She blinked at them all, reminding herself of all the rats (hundreds of rats) she'd relegated to soggy fields, and then she joined the fray, hugging and laughing with all her friends who had made the trek from the city.

By ten-thirty, Mona was drunk and stoned. She went to the bathroom and in the time it took her to pee the house somehow became too crowded. Everywhere she looked people talked over each other loudly or shrieked with feigned laughter, mouths gaping, vacant eyes. Holding on to the wooden frames of the walls for support, she wandered upstairs and found more people (more people, everywhere more people) gathered in a little crowd in the turret room. Mona hadn't been there since Heidi set up the studio and now she was surprised to see finished paintings leaning against the walls: blocks of color tracking across a canvas that reminded her of a Frankenthaler except without the precise, satisfying mess; an Alice Neel-esque portrait; a bright blue Hockney pool. People were nodding seriously and among them Mona saw Florence, from her undergrad BFA program, leaning in to look more closely at the Alice Neel knock-off. Last month Florence had been at a residency in Wyoming and next month her work would appear in a group show in Tokyo (facts Mona had gathered, regretfully, from social media).

Heidi was explaining to everyone that she'd set herself the challenge of replicating a hundred great paintings, one for every year of the last century. She'd already finished passable versions of a Mondrian and Schiele and a Hopper, she said, gesturing to paintings Mona hadn't even noticed. Now she was working on a smaller (but to scale) *El Guernica*. Florence told Heidi to be sure to document her progress, and that the project could use its own Instagram account.

"What about, like, originality? Authenticity?" Mona asked. She felt unsteady on her feet and leaned against the doorframe as she spoke, her skin as inflamed as a sunburn, the skin on her face tight and loose at the same time. She swallowed a hiccup.

"Isn't that the entire point of the project?" Florence asked.

"What is?" Mona said.

"That authenticity is an outmoded concept. That to wrestle with the issues of our day we need to recycle thought itself," Florence said. To Mona this seemed almost entirely wrong.

"But doesn't replicating an outmoded canon just reestablish its power?" Mona asked.

"Or it brings attention to the way the entire concept of a canon is absurd. Like, it's creating a funhouse image of the canon, you know?" Florence used air quotes on the word canon.

"Yes, that's it! You really understand this, Florence," Heidi said. The room fell quiet as everyone absorbed the martial grey of the miniature Picasso in progress; Mona alone was looking at Heidi. For a brief, chilling moment, as Mona watched, the ghost's face turned into a skull. Chunks of putrid skin fell from her cheeks and her dark hair was long and tangled and half rotting, like hair pulled in clumps from the drain. Then she was back to normal, breaking the silence, saying, "My Mix-Ups are my first love, but I was interested in trying something new. You'd be surprised at how much changing your perspective can lead to generative work. You should try it, Mona."

Of course Mona took Heidi's advice. With a bottle of wine and a joint, she went up to the attic. Noise was muffled up there and soon she forgot entirely about the party downstairs. She started slowly, moving Heidi's assemblages around and wiping the dust onto her pants. Then she began painting. She painted and painted, oblivious to the drips she left on the floor. Hours passed; she peed into a jar. She painted until her hand cramped and she switched hands and kept painting. When Jim looked for her the next afternoon, shouting her name throughout the house, she was disheveled, almost unrecognizable, but she'd finished her first important work.

"Mona? Are you okay? This was the last place I thought you'd be," he said, side-hugging her. It had only been twelve hours but she'd already forgotten the way his body generated warmth, the way his body was a familiar animal.

"Look what I did," she said, sweeping her arm out to encompass Heidi's Mix-Ups, all of them now entirely covered with paint.

The new layer on top of the sculptures gave them a strange energy; crouched together in the stuffy attic they were uncanny, almost alive. Everywhere there were odd limbs and juts and rounded things that looked like bellies, the paint on top forming a kind of skin. The one that had been Heidi's favorite, with the flowerpot, was painted a pinkish-taupe with dark splotches that gave it a rakish look. Each of the Mix-Ups were entirely unrecognizable from their former selves; she had transformed them, like an alchemist, into new, odd things, devoid of all context. Here it was, finally—something Mona had unearthed from her obtuse, unyielding interior. Something she could show the world.

A Way to Find You
by KB Ballentine

A crust of moon slices
the dawn, clouds furrowing
first lavender then peach
before robin's egg blue perches
the horizon. My future
hangs in the balance, strangers
nibbling my profile, uninterested
in living, only in scrolling
through yesterday's choices.
Sun brightens, gulps
what's left of night,
and I abandon the bed, mourning
sleep. My cousin lingers
partly in the Gulf Stream, partly
in Ohio's soil, but always in the stars.

   We are starlight, stardust
sharing the sequined constellations,
the meteor's flash, the solstice
where we can stand still. At the edge
of everything, the self
we've tried all along to avoid:

   Here is where we'll meet.

Interview with a Ghost
by Timothy Arliss OBrien

In the moonlit shadows, I met a specter,
A spirit from realms beyond, a ghost, a reflector.
With whispers and echoes, a call from the past,
A spectral interview, an encounter vast.

In the haunted hollows, where memories lie,
I summoned the apparition, beneath the midnight sky.
A wisp of the ethereal, a presence untold,
The ghost materialized, a tale to unfold.

I asked the phantom, "What secrets do you keep?
In the realm of the departed, where shadows sleep?"
The ghost sighed softly, a breeze through the air,
"I carry tales of sorrow, of joy, and despair."

"Once I walked the Earth, with a beating heart,
Now I'm but a whisper, a memory torn apart.
I haunt in the echoes of laughter and of tears,
In the corridors of time, where the past so often reappears."

"Tell me," I implore, "of the journey beyond,
Of the mysteries of death, where souls dawned."
The ghost spoke of a passage, a cosmic tide,
To realms unknown, there is no guide.

"In the tapestry of existence, life and death entwine,
A dance eternal, an otherworldly shrine.
I've glimpsed the cosmic soup, a recipe with care,
Where every ingredient is a soul, stirred in with prayer."

The ghost's words haunted me and danced in the night,
A lyrical symphony, a spectral light.

In the interview with the beyond, questions unfurl,
As the ghost whispered secrets from the otherworld.

As the clock struck midnight, the apparition faded,
Back to the shadows, hopefully not to return unpersuaded.

The interview with the ghost, a poetic trance,
A glimpse into the afterlife, a spectral dance.

Q&A portion

Timothy: In the twilight realm between worlds, I find myself in the company of a ghost. Thank you for joining us tonight. Could you share a bit about who you were in life?

Ghost: In life, I was a wanderer, a seeker of dreams. My name has been lost to time, but my essence lingers in the echoes of the places I once called home.

Timothy: What led you to linger in the realm beyond, rather than moving on to whatever lies ahead?

Ghost: Unfinished business, a tale left untold. A connection to the mortal realm tethers me here, as I navigate the corridors of existence that intertwine the living and the departed.

Timothy: Can you describe the nature of your existence now? How do you experience the passage of time?

Ghost: Time is a vast tapestry, and I am but a thread within it. I witness the ebb and flow of moments, reliving fragments of the past, yet unable to grasp the present. I am a spectator in the grand theater of existence.

Timothy: Are there others like you in this spectral realm? Do you interact with them, or is your existence solitary?

Ghost: Solitude is my constant companion, but occasionally, I encounter other lost souls adrift in this ethereal sea. We share silent nods of understanding, acknowledging the shared burden of being caught between worlds.

Timothy: Is there a message or wisdom you wish to impart to the living, a lesson learned from your transition to this afterlife?

Ghost: Cherish the fleeting moments, for time is a river that never ceases to flow. The thread of life is delicate, and each breath contributes to its intricate beauty. Live with purpose, and let your echoes resonate long after your footsteps fade.

Timothy: How do you perceive the living when you observe them? Is there a longing or a sense of connection?

Ghost: I see them as fleeting flames, casting ephemeral shadows. There is a longing, an ache for the warmth of the living, for the tangible touch of the world I once called home. Yet, I am but a silent observer, a whisper in the winds of memory.

Timothy: If there were a way for you to find peace or closure, what form would that take?

Ghost: Peace lies in the resolution of my unfinished story. To find closure, I yearn for the living to discover the truths I left untold, to unravel the mysteries of life that bind me to this spectral existence.

Timothy: Thank you for sharing a glimpse of your existence with us. As we part ways, may you find solace in the currents that carry you through the realms beyond.

Ghost: And may your journey through the mortal realm be filled with purpose and understanding. Until we meet again, in the dance of shadows and light.

Sleeping In
by Gabby Gilliam

Lawrence Raab said sleep
is a way to stave off death.

Maybe that's what I'm doing
on these long mornings

when the dawn light tries to creep
beneath my blackout curtains.

Last night's tears leaving
my skin starched and stiff

and photos of you the first things
that appear when I unlock my phone.

My body is protecting itself,
afraid I'll catch your death,

so my leaden limbs pull the sheet back
up to my chin and I dream you back to life.

Miles of Ghosts
by Gurupreet K. Khalsa

And miles of ghosts beneath our sleep.
—Philip Metres, *Song for Refugees*

Beneath our sleep we juggle gold
and crimson fruit of cackling djinns
twirling insouciant fingers bold.

Beneath our sleep we flounder, spin
in roils of black and endless waves
where circling monsters lurk within.

Beneath our sleep, stumbling in caves
of blackened tunnels, massed ghosts dent
pillars of safety, opening graves.

Beneath our sleep we're spent, lament
the days of order passed, unease
as road map burns, illusion bent.

Beneath our sleep, we seek release,
a path to certainty and peace.

Around the House
by James B. Nicola

They said in ancient Greece and Rome and such
locales—and maybe everywhere, I guess—
that household gods—say, ancestors'—would look
upon us in the home, as from an urn
with ashes in it on a mantelpiece—
or even absent ashes or the vase.

But I have my Italian grandfather's
old grooming scissors, made when things would last,
and use them still when trimming eyebrows back
or other facial hair, and think of him
gone now these fifty years. And turning sixty
is the small stool, a fold-up job, a child's,
with slatted top, just big enough to fit
a mug and magazine: my German "Pa"
mailed up my brothers and me each a stool
the Christmas I was five. And under each
he'd etched our nicknames in clean, slanted caps,
the very penmanship the envelopes
of letters sported, like Roy Lichtenstein's
captions or thought balloons. JIMINY CRICKET.

Both objects, after years of stalwart service,
are silent as the spirits of a home
in Greece; larēs or penatēs, in Rome.

Icicles Before Spring
by Lynette Esposito

Ghosts point their cold fingers
down from the roof--
long narrow prisms holding light
then gone.
The sun
understands their chilly spirit—
encourages them to dance==
then with a quick tempo--
drip drip crack=
a strong spring breath
frees them from their perch
like a maestro's baton
counting a beat.

Halloween Still Life With
by Aletha Irby

Straw-bodied
Corpse
Alarmingly
Red-headed, sporting his Rockabilly pompadour;
Effigy gangly-toothed,
Cropped, and
Rickety after the manner of Rumpelstiltskin:
Overalls ransacked from the ragbag by ramshackle moonlight,
Warding away zombie-feathered crows.

NOPPERO-BO
by Dee Allen

His steel *katana*
Cleaves its way
Through air swiftly
Like a dragonfly
Through would-be
Thieves and killers
With their lustful
Eyes set on a
Single woman in a
Crimson silk *kimono*
Carnation-pink sash
Around her waist
Alone and defenceless
But primarily on
Her ribboned purse
Full of *ryo*—

A stillborn crime—
A bright stream
Of loosened blood—
A scattered mess
Of dead fools—

The lone *samurai*
On horseback
Rides off, hoofbeats
Kicking up dust,
Only to turn
Around and offer
The young woman
A mounted ride home.
As she steps closer
To accept his unspoken
Offer, her thanks,
The woman takes her
Horsebound protector by the

Transparent hand,
Confronting him face

To no face—

Noppero-bo: Japanese: "Faceless phantom."
Ryo: A gold currency unit used in ancient Japan before 19th Century American contact.

Imponderable
by Ann Howells

*What is the difference between fog
and cloud, vision and ectoplasm?*

I lean into vapor, into you,
planchette straining to letters of your name.
I am candleflame, spark and flicker, votive.
You are ghost, opalescent and translucent.
Hovering mist. Virga.
I see you in winter breath,
    steam rising like a promise from my cup.
I carry your heart in my throat.

Awake
by Cynthia Graae

How had the intruder gotten in? Not through the deadbolted door to our fourth-story apartment. Not through the windows. I couldn't see his face. Our bedroom was too dark. My husband was thirty miles away at Johns Hopkins Hospital on a ventilator with a tube down his throat. To prevent him from reflexively yanking out the tube, his hands were strapped to his bed. His heart had been failing for months. He couldn't help me.

I wanted to spend the night in the chair beside him, but his cardiologist had sent me home. "You'll need your rest," he said. The future tense, as if he were speaking a warning. I thought I'd be too exhausted to sleep when I got home, especially after I'd stopped for gas at an all-night convenience store where men hanging around the pumps were drinking and shooting up. But I fell asleep the moment I turned out the light.

And now I was wide awake, staring at the intruder who stood at the foot of my bed.

The red digits of my clock glowed three-twenty a.m.

The intruder lay down on top of me so gently that, in my fatigue, I had no urge to scream or fight back. He seemed weightless. I remember how odd that was until I felt his hair fall onto my face. I recognized the feathery touch. Relieved. I said, Oh, it's you.

Immediately, I regretted it. He vanished as silently as he'd arrived. I was positive that by addressing him directly, I had violated the laws governing night travel across great distances and through walls.

He was my best friend, my lover, my personal stand-up comic, my gourmet chef. We became parents and learned to become adults together. The moments we had with each other now were as precious as our first days of falling in love decades earlier. Carelessly, I had just lost one of those moments.

I couldn't stop myself from crying, Please come back.

Another violation I realized too late. I had closed off all possibility that he could return.

He needs me, I thought. He must be in trouble. I lifted the phone, which made no sense.

I didn't believe in religion, an afterlife, god, telepathy, ESP, supernatural phenomena, or motion that didn't follow the laws of gravity, so I scolded myself, Don't be dramatic, He isn't weightless. He can't travel through walls. He is thirty miles away. You were dreaming.

That was hard to believe. I regarded myself as something of an expert on dreams. Eight years earlier, I'd recorded mine faithfully, several a night, in an effort to teach myself the art of lucid dreaming, a state of dreaming in which you are aware that you are dreaming and not, as dreams can fool you into thinking, flying to Europe on an elephant. Dreams warped reality that way. By keeping a dream journal, I'd learned to recognize their signs, pygmy animals napping on chairs, for example, and extra rooms I'd wanted but hadn't been there before. Dreams sometimes argue back. When a dream mugger insisted he was real, I grabbed his head and tore him down the middle as if he were a character in a comic book. Dream, I said. His fragments floated to the gutter. Like that dream mugger, my emotions told me that my husband really transported himself to our bedroom. Not a dream, they insisted. If my husband's visit had been a dream, they reminded me, the shape of our bedroom would have been distorted, I would have shouted Dream instead of Oh, it's you, and—a really tell-tale sign. I would have woken up when he disappeared, not—as I'd done—when he arrived.

Logic of course, still insisted that my husband's appearance was a dream. Everything I knew about science told me that he not have made a nighttime visit to our bedroom.

And when my emotions became aware they were losing

their battle with rationality, they yelled, If you aren't going to phone the hospital, at least write down what happened. It will be concrete evidence that your husband visited you at three-twenty a.m.

If I'd remembered my dream journal entry the night before my brother's heart attack eight years earlier, I might have searched for a pen.

* * *

Eight years earlier.

My brother's heart attack took me and the rest of my family by surprise. He was only forty-nine. At the time I didn't know him well. He was ten when I'd gone away to college. We hadn't lived near each other since then. Even our vacation homes were hundreds of miles apart. In those days, long-distance phone calls were expensive. We didn't make them.

My brother's heart attack was massive. It damaged so much tissue that doctors placed him in a medically induced coma, nearly motionless. I drove five hundred miles to spend a few hours next to his dormant body. I parked my dark blue Ford Explorer in his driveway beside his car, which, to my surprise, was a black Explorer, the same year and model as mine. Although it would have been rational to believe that our cars were nearly identical by coincidence, I found myself stroking his Explorer as if it were a relic of a mythical saint I didn't believe in.

Two months later, after I'd returned home, my brother awoke from his coma, he and I spoke by phone. He told me that he'd realized he was having a heart attack when he was in his Explorer on his way to a construction site he supervised. He had driven to a gas station and asked the attendants to phone 911. He also told me that upon awakening from his coma, he had a vivid memory of leaving his life.

I lost my fear of dying, he said. Leaving was peaceful. I

don't know why I decided to return to life. When I mentioned this to my surgeon, he told me that technically I died on the operating table and that he'd been amazed he could revive me.

Because fear of my own death often showed up in my dreams, my brother's near-death experience spurred me to reread my journal. I had no memory of my dream the night my brother had his heart attack—it certainly hadn't worried me, the way some dreams did. But there, in my own handwriting, were the key elements of my brother's heart attack story:

> I was…in my Ford Explorer….Every time I came to what looked like a gas station, it was nonexistent or closed. I tried to call the police. The phone was on the wall. I wondered if I should call 911.

Within minutes of discovering that dream, I telephoned my brother. What do you think? I asked.

You shouldn't dream, he said in a tone that made me realize he was remembering his out-of-body experience.

It was a coincidence, I laughed.

From five hundred miles away, I felt his equilibrium shake.

* * *

But, as I said, the night the intruder visited me, I wasn't thinking about my brother or that dream. It was far too long ago. I was focused on my husband who was suffering on a ventilator at Johns Hopkins. And as his cardiologist had said, to face what was coming, I needed rest. I didn't call the hospital. I didn't write anything down. I rolled onto my side and went back to sleep.

Only to be jolted by the ringing phone. My alarm clock now read five-thirty.

A doctor on duty in coronary care said, Two hours ago, your husband took a turn for the worse. His blood pressure dropped, and his fever spiked. She wanted permission to open his neck to find the source of the fever.

My whole being screamed, Two hours ago, he needed me. I should have driven to the hospital or at least telephoned. I don't want him to suffer needlessly. He should be participating in the decision about whether to operate.

In a quandary, I phoned his cardiologist.

Operating is our only hope, he said. He asked me to meet him at his hospital office.

I rushed to Baltimore, parked the car, and raced to his office. He hadn't arrived, so I sat on the bench where my husband and I had so often waited for his appointment. Near a window close by, there was a night-blooming cereus, a plant that bloomed only at night and only once a year. My husband and I had watched its growth for months. As I waited for the cardiologist, I walked to the window. As if the cereus bore witness to my husband's waning life, its bloom, from only hours before, was already wilting.

The cardiologist's arrival startled me from my reverie. Surgery hadn't revealed the cause of my husband's fever. I understood that we were out of options. Ventilators weren't for long-term life support. My husband would be disconnected within a day or two, the cardiologist said. Sooner, if I thought that was best.

Blind with grief, I stumbled through the labyrinthine corridors to the coronary care unit. How many dozens of times had my husband and I been in the all-too-familiar hospital? It was our second home. I called our daughter, who lived an hour away and had visited almost every day.

My husband was awake and straining to free himself from the tube in his throat. I told him he could choose to be taken off the ventilator after our daughter arrived. But, I emphasized, that would mean saying goodbye. I asked if that was what he wanted.

Soon, he signaled yes with his eyes.

I asked again to be sure.

A nurse arrived with extra sedation to protect him from pain and panic when the breathing tube was removed. I felt as if I'd lied to him because I didn't know how drugged he would be. Friends and family members appeared. By the time our daughter reached his bedside, he could no longer respond to a hand squeeze or blink his eyes—we had robbed him of the chance to say goodbye

We held him and told him we loved him. Our daughter, not a disbeliever like me, sang "Come Unto Him" from *Messiah*, her soprano voice at first wavering and then brave as she reached "All ye who labor and are weary." Doctors and nurses congregated to listen. Every nerve in my body prayed to whatever power might respond, Please let him hear her. Simultaneously, I pleaded to the sedation, Please stop his pain, even if that means he won't know we're here.

A nurse disconnected monitors, the feeding and hydration tubes, the ventilator last. Gently, as if he were a baby bird, she fitted an oxygen mask on him. I prayed again, this time to him: as you leave us, may your journey, like the one my brother almost took, bring you peace.

His breathing shallowed. Within a minute he was gone.

I understood what reason could not explain. He was nearby, not yet a memory. He could not return. However ephemeral his visit had been the night before, it was as real as my life. Deep in my heart or wherever emotions reside, the still-palpable feeling of him lying weightless on top of me, his hair caressing my face, would forever be our goodbye.

You Know It's Coming
by Molly O'Dell

As soon as August heat breaks, weather
becomes a drug, pulls us deep

into the woods along the riverbank
otters romp and roll in the cool stream.

Pallid walnut leaves fall from brittle
stems where children wait on the school bus.

Silky cobwebs cluster in porch corners
& branches we bushwhack early mornings.

Temperatures collude with broccoli, kale & bok choy
dew re-appears, suddenly, when wet air

cools enough to sweat again. Evening light
peels away every speck of haze.

Walnuts and their rachises litter the yard,
maggots magically emerge from nutshells.

Only witch hazel's left to pollinate,
veins on leaves shuttle yellow & red

into their blades precisely the way an artist's
brush kaleidoscopes every tree in town.

Cooler nights & a basket of butternut squash
catapults my lover to daybreak delight

then orange lit pumpkins watch a metallic bone
ghost squeak & bang with every movement at the door.

Imagined
by Valerie Hunter

Lea discovers the photograph
while sorting through the layers
of Granddad's life, cleaning
the mess that so many years of living
leaves behind. Wedged in the seam
of a cardboard box, a black and white
picture of a little boy—dark hair,
round cheeks, wide mouth.
As soon as Lea sees him, she can hear
his voice in her head, his wild laugh,
can feel her own rising panic.

She passes the photo to her grandmother,
asks who he is, knows the answer will differ
from the one in her own head. Grandma
shakes her head, then flips the picture over,
her expression shifting to sadness
as she reads the name written there.
"That's your granddad's brother Nicholas."
The name hits Lea like a projectile,
but she forces her voice steady.
"I didn't know Granddad had a brother."

"He died young, probably not long
after this picture was taken. Pneumonia,
I think, or maybe flu? Your granddad never
talked about him, it hit him so hard;
I only know from your great aunt Pat."

Lea nods and nods, as though
this simple motion will keep her
from screaming, will keep her heart
in her chest. She tells herself
she must have seen this picture before
(even though her grandmother clearly hadn't),
must have heard the name from someone
(even though Granddad had been

too heartbroken to speak of him,
and Lea had never met Great Aunt Pat).
Surely there is a logical explanation,
some far-fetched truth to cling to.

But all she knows for sure
is that she played with Nicky
every day when she was five,
got upset when Mom referred to him
as imaginary, clung to his hand
as he dragged her into all nature
of thrilling adventures.
She knew everything about him—
he loved caterpillars but was scared
of butterflies, he could read better than
she could, he didn't know any of the songs
she'd learned in kindergarten, but he'd let
her teach him, his voice always slightly
off-key when he sang. Now she realizes
how little she actually knows—about him,
about herself, about the nature of imagination
and the slipperiness of death—
and she wants so badly to call him back
and beg him to explain.

A HAUNTED HOUSE
by Sarah Das Gupta

In the House only sound
A few notes of Chopin in the night
Voices echo and drift in old walls
Imprisoned perhaps for centuries
A dog whines from the attic
The sound wavering, plaintive
Water's still running in the old pantry
A skipping rope thumps insistently
High above on the nursery floor
Tennis balls thud on ghostly racquets
In tournaments long forgotten

In the kitchen bells summon
Maids to empty rooms
Footsteps sound in the hall
Never arrive at the door
Cricket bats boys have left
For Waterloo, the Somme, Burma
'It's a long way to Tipperary'
They'll not return at all.

Upholstery Geist
by Abbie Doll

Poltergeist – German origin, "knocking ghost".

You're not going to believe me, but we got geisted, geisted good and hard. But before we get into that, why don't we start from scratch.

I've never been a fan of fabrics that conceal—shower curtains especially, for all the obvious insert-horror-film-scene-here reasons, but I don't like my windows covered either; so I suppose, yeah, my beef lies exclusively with curtains. Lace, cotton, silk, the fabric itself doesn't matter; it's the veil they create that I don't trust. The inherent secrecy. If there's a window, I want to see beyond the glass; I shouldn't have to peel a wrinkled burlap sack off the pane to see my front lawn. That's the whole purpose of the window—to let me look out without feeling trapped inside—which let's face it, most days, we are in one sense or another. I don't want the distorted cottony view; I want the unadulterated green of suburbia, the fresh sunrise shooting straight through, obliterating my retinas. It's better than a piping hot double espresso, I kid you not.

But here's the thing. I got married last month (thank you, thank you, I know it's great but please get a grip and hold your applause so that I can continue without further interruption). Anyway, one of the compromises my wife insisted I make—well now that I think about it, it's the only one—is that we put up some g-d drapes in this naked house. I just so happened to prefer it barren, but that's what my sex life's going to become if I don't cooperate, and we can't have that. I don't have to tell you why. You get it.

Untended urges lead down dark paths. Okay, there, I went and told you.

*

The second we came home from the honeymoon, she dove headfirst into this manic project—sculpted a whole week out of jotting down the window dimensions, dragging us to every store in a fifty-mile radius that sold fabrics, rings, and rods. All the accoutrements, you get the picture. She was happier than a ref in the World Cup final to make the calls, and I was happy to let her, happy, in the interest of total honesty, to be relieved of this high-stakes hassle. My wife spent half our time abroad admiring gauche floral sun dresses, anyway, dreaming of the perfect discreet manner in which she could successfully strip them off the tourists she was spying on without them noticing. Hell, I'm pretty sure she, given the chance, would've hung them in the windows as is, bodies included.

She dreamt of sheer perfection and wasted many of our beachside hours running her fingers down her own dresses—manipulating the folds of the fabric until all the tension, ridges, and rivulets met her many, many tough-to-please standards.

Watching her sit there in that trancelike state, it occurred to me, that okay, maybe she's a little loony. I know, I know, we're not supposed to say that nowadays (sure as hell shouldn't be devoting it to a fresh-from-the-church spouse), but please, allow me to demonstrate my point—the woman was obsessed.

And it didn't stop there. Things were about to get a lot weirder.

Look, we'd tied the proverbial knot already, what was I supposed to do? To be honest, I'm shocked she didn't insist on sporting a sheer voile as her wedding gown. I half-expected her to shapeshift into a curtain herself; one minute, she'd be standing there beside me, and the next, merrily swaying in the window.

Okay, so fast forward to a literal warehouse of boxes popping up on our front porch, as if we'd just become major investors in Walmart and now were stuck housing a percentage of their merchandise to prove our loyalty beyond financial measures. Don't mention this to her, but it felt as though we'd become hoarders overnight; cardboard and curtains sprawled all over my once-pristine, modest residence.

    You should've seen her when that first box arrived though. Her eyes were downright glowing, but it didn't stop there; you could see the jittery anticipation extend over her inflated cheeks and bottom-bit lip. She gutted that first box like some fresh-caught bass, turned her attention to me, and insisted we christen the curtains she clenched, slimy guts dripping out between her knuckles. Yes, it's precisely what you're imagining, and yes, there was a peculiar and unsettling urgency to it, but I wasn't about to protest. Besides, she was still clutching the box cutter; my cardboard skin might've been next. She spread the daisy-ridden black panel out onto the hardwood in front of our parlor's gaping three-pane window, disrobed, and beckoned me over.

    I hate to admit it now, but the first thing I noticed then was how cute she looked wrapped up like a steamy, fleshy burrito. And to be quite frank with you, I was hungry. So, go ahead and sue me if you're going to, but I slept with my wife right there for all the world to see. And we weren't concerned with hiding what was happening. Quite the opposite. Our circus-level efforts were on proud display.

    Night after night, we kept going at it, repeating the process at every other window in the house. Same exact order, she'd slice open a box and sprawl across the floor, waiting for me to follow her into the folds of our newly wedded passion.

    Sure, it was weird as hell, there was no denying that, but something about it got me going. Yes, there was nudity, yes, sure, cleavage, that's always a contributing factor, but there was something about this eerie-yet-alluring act of her formally marrying us to our domestic décor that roused me into a frenzy. And hey, it's not my fault she went with silk and handpicked every bold color that accentuated her exposed skin. She had a real knack for it, let me tell you. Almost like she'd been born to seduce.

    Anyway, who says fabric can't be erotic? It succeeds when it's on the body so why not off? She was opening me up to this new world, which sure as hell made me appreciate the rooms in our home that much more…here's where we…and over there's where we…

Use your imagination, you creep. I'm not spilling the in-between-the-sheets deets of our sex life. Some sense of privacy, for my sanity and your own, must be maintained.

But let's just say, the curtains quickly morphed into these beautiful manifestations of our love; they even started to look infused with it, as though someone had sewn our passion on and now we got to admire our disembodied desire. Our bodies, too, began to feel embroidered, and we came to recognize each meticulous, sensual stitch in each other's skin.

*

But surprise, surprise, the bliss didn't last. It never does.

The very second the last window was covered and christened, our marathon of lovemaking ceased. But the memories we'd forged were still there and still very much present; I wasted countless hours watching them drift around in the light breeze from the cracked windows, taunting me as reminders of happier days.

Even worse, when I tried to reminisce with her, she acted as if none of it ever happened, as if we hadn't spent hours upon hours wrapped up together in those curtains like tousled sheets. I pleaded and pleaded with her. *Couldn't we reupholster every piece of furniture in the house too? There has to be some other project you're willing to pursue.* I craved her, craved her interior design expertise, needed her to continue injecting color and life into me, this renovated bachelor.

The changes weren't restricted to her new lack of arousal though. As soon as we were done with what she set out to do, the house knew, too. I started hearing all these disembodied knocks on the walls. Thick thuds left by enraged fists.

As if the curtains remembered.

She insisted I was losing it. *We've never made love on the floor, that's ridiculous.*

She was so emphatically insistent that I started questioning the durability of my own sanity. I was certain that's how our marriage had begun. A thousand percent certain, but this new phase was so drastically different that I could no longer claim to know much of anything.

And the knocks grew worse. Louder.

Closer.

They started to keep me up at night, and I got the sense that they siphoned enjoyment from my sleep deprivation, whatever they were. It started playful but soon developed a malignant twist. The second I grew sleepy enough to conk out, there it was. A loud knock on the headboard, directly above my forehead. Followed by one on the slab at my feet.

The knocks would continue, climbing up to the ceiling, knocking every second or so but with no reliable regularity—like a broken metronome.

It was maddening. Some were soft and enticing, the next thunderous and threatening.

I told my wife the house was unhappy with us, displeased with her sudden disinterest and the resulting lack of fornication. I mean, as you know, I was too, but the house was more adept at verbalizing its needs. It didn't wait around for a well-timed opportunity to vocalize its concerns, didn't waste energy trying to placate her sour moods. It wailed like a toddler with a perpetual tantrum, and I was the lone parent left to tend to the sobs, the screams, and all the pounding, pounding, pounding.

My wife went about her life as if nothing had changed, everything was normal, went on as if her sex drive had been permanently sated, almost as if she'd never possessed one to begin with.

Meanwhile, the house proceeded to grow worse…and worse…

What started as knocks, soon departed the auditory realm and grew physical.

Those damn curtains started to mess with me. Whenever my wife wasn't looking or I found myself alone in a room, they'd slither around my wrist, grab at my hair, brush the nape of my neck—each and every place neglected since the fabrics were first hung. It was as though our love itself had been exorcised and now hung there in the window, on display for the benefit of the neighborhood but never again for us ourselves. Maybe that'd been the crux of her intention all along—staging appearances.

And I'd be lying if I didn't admit to *some* arousal, but it was a biological response, plain and simple; I couldn't help it, couldn't control it. All those now-distant memories had me stopping and staring at the drapes any time I entered a room. Hell, I could still see my wife's naked frame cozily swirled in their folds, can you blame me for half-expecting her to pop out from behind?

The imagination and the subconscious get unruly. Unmet needs, as I've said.

So yes, the curtains were nice for a time, but not for any of the reasons we anticipated. She was right, they improved the aesthetic of the place, but don't you dare tell her I said that.

I was deprived. Deprived of attention, touch, affection, you name it, I craved it. So please, I'm begging you, don't judge me too hard for what happened next.

*

It was months later, when our dry spell had ceased to be a spell and had expanded into a massive, barren desert—wrinkled sand every which way you look with no end in sight. I loved my wife with such ferocity, but bodies have basic needs and when those needs go not just unmet but to the point of complete neglect, well…

I walked into the living room one night and spotted her

diaphanous, lace-clad figure standing there looking out into the backyard. I approached and went to lean in, but as I did, the mirage of her dissolved into the maroon drapes we'd hung together so long ago. But I still felt her presence, somehow, still felt her there with me, as she'd been back then.

There was a firm knock on the wall; it made a hollow echo.

It happened again and again, until the repetition grew insistent. Demanding. Forceful.

Next thing I know, the bloody fabric's got me, anaconda-coiled around my waist. Slams me up against the wall, cracking the plaster, cracking my skull. But I let it happen. That same desire, all those urges I'd been swallowing for months was there, blooming. I felt it in the room, same as anything, and it matched the sentiments I carried—but with an aggression I'd ignored up until now.

It made me realize, I was mad. All this time, I'd been resenting my wife, whom I still considered brand new, wishing she was under warranty, or that I was under literally any other circumstance at the moment.

All that angst got the better of me and I yanked the drapes off, let the rod clatter upon the floor. I wanted my window view back. I wanted my wife back, my contentment, my satisfaction. All of it.

But they fought back. Knocked me against the wall again and again until they'd had their way, and I'd be lying if I said there wasn't a part of me that found substantial relief from the whole thing.

I felt exorcised. It didn't matter that my nose was smashed, didn't matter that there was blood trailing down my chin and neck and onto what had until now been a stain-free shirt. Whatever drops were atop the drapes, you couldn't see them; the color match was out of this world, as if she'd foreseen this too.

I passed in and out of consciousness to that same tiresome repetition of fists hammering, pounding, slamming, nailing me into the ground, pummeling my existence out of me and into the floorboards for all I knew, but I was so starved for physical attention that the only thing I could think in my mind was, *thank you, thank you, thank you,* and I looked up out the window admiring the snow falling, flakes glittering against the warm glow stemming from the porch light, and I lay there, overwhelmed by a wave of gratitude of all things, and the release of everything in my spirit that had been so unbelievably pent up, jammed, and congested. Despite the brutality of my reality, there was a downright spiritual stillness to the moment, an undeniable warmth in that instant of peace, and my adrenaline, lucky me, was still high enough to block out all the pain, shame, and heartbreak that'd inevitably follow, crashing into me as though the entire structure of the house had collapsed and buried me beneath.

The Holiday Kitchen
by Lynette Esposito

Cauldron smoke rises

like gray ghosts dancing --

Translucent gossamer beings

seeking escape from the boil.

Twisted fingers

torture them into the air--

 higher and higher

until first one, then all

disappear.

Out of the black more come,

souls flying like eyeless insects, grotesque

but free

because of the Christmas soup.

The Shortest Night
by KB Ballentine

Sky polished, the mirror of night
   blinks its button-lights, twilight
surrendering to the shock
       of crescent moon. An owl spooks
the cedars leaning with the wind,
   upper branches creaking in the hickories.
What can't be seen in midsummer shadow
     is the latch that locks the phantoms
of past desires. Stare into this darkness.
   The gate is barred – for now.
Let the dormouse sleep and the hare hide
      as they will. Watch midnight sneak in,
tiptoe through fog filling the fields.
   Don't lose your way.

BIOS

DEE ALLEN
African-Italian performance poet based in Oakland, California. Active on creative writing & Spoken Word since the early 1990s. Author of 8 books-- *Boneyard, Unwritten Law, Stormwater, Skeletal Black* [all from POOR Press], *Elohi Unitsi* [Conviction 2 Change Publishing], *Rusty Gallows: Passages Against Hate* [Vagabond Books], *Plans* [Nomadic Press] and coming in February 2024, *Crimson Stain* [EYEPUBLISHEWE]--and 71 anthology appearances under his figurative belt so far.

KB BALLENTINE
KB Ballentine began writing poetry so she could better understand how to teach it to her high school students. Since then she has been drawn to the light and spirit of poetry and has left that ill-fated novel in the bottom drawer – where it belongs! Learn more at www.kbballentine.com.

CHRISTOPHER BARNES
In 1998 Christopher Barnes won a Northern Arts writers award. In July 2000 he read at Waterstones bookshop to promote the anthology 'Titles Are Bitches'. Christmas 2001 he debuted at Newcastle's famous Morden Tower doing a reading of poems. Each year he read for Proudwords lesbian and gay writing festival and partook in workshops. 2005 saw the publication of his collection LOVEBITES published by Chanticleer Press, 6/1 Jamaica Mews, Edinburgh.
On Saturday 16Th August 2003 he read at the Edinburgh Festival as a Per Verse.
Christmas 2001 The Northern Cultural Skills Partnership sponsored him to be mentored by Andy Croft in conjunction with New Writing North. He made a radio programme for Web FM community radio about his writing group. October-November 2005, he entered a poem/visual image into the art exhibition The Art Cafe Project, his piece Post-Mark was shown in Betty's Newcastle. This event was sponsored by Pride On The Tyne. He made a digital film with artists Kate Sweeney and Julie Ballands at a film making workshop called Out Of The Picture which was shown at the festival party for Proudwords, it contains his poem The Old Heave-Ho. He worked on a collaborative art and literature project called How Gay Are Your Genes, facilitated by Lisa Mathews (poet) which exhibited at The Hatton Gallery, Newcastle University, including a film piece by the artist Predrag Pajdic in which he read his poem On Brenkley St. The event was funded by The

Policy, Ethics and Life Sciences Research Institute, Bio-science Centre at Newcastle's Centre for Life. He was involved in the Five Arts Cities poetry postcard event which exhibited at The Seven Stories children's literature building. In May he had 2006 a solo art/poetry exhibition at The People's Theatre.

CALLIE S. BLACKSTONE
Callie S. Blackstone writes both poetry and prose. Her debut chapbook *sing eternal* is available through Bottlecap Press. Her online home is calliesblackstone.com.

KAI BROACH
Kai Broach (he/they) writes fiction and poetry. Their work has appeared in *Jeopardy*, *Scribendi*, and *Deep Overstock*. They live in Portland, Oregon, where they offer literary and bathroom advice to the customers of Powell's Books.

ROGER CAMP
Roger Camp is the author of three photography books including the award winning *Butterflies in Flight*, Thames & Hudson, 2002 and Heat, Charta, Milano, 2008. His work has appeared in numerous journals including *The New England Review*, *Witness* and the *New York Quarterly*. Represented by the Robin Rice Gallery, NYC, more of his work may be seen on Luminous-Lint.com.

MICKEY COLLINS
Mickey ~~rights wrongs~~. Mickey ~~wrongs rites~~. Mickey writes words, sometimes wrong words but he tries to get it write.

ABBIE DOLL
Abbie Doll is a writer residing in Columbus, OH, with an MFA from Lindenwood University and is a fiction editor at *Identity Theory*. Her work has been featured or is forthcoming in *Door Is a Jar Magazine*, *The Bitchin' Kitsch*, and *Ellipsis Zine*, among others. Connect on socials @AbbieDollWrites.

CHRISTINE ESKILSON
I write short mystery fiction. My stories have appeared in a number of magazines and anthologies, including *Best New England Crime Stories* and *Malice Domestic*, and I received awards in the Al Blanchard Short Crime Fiction Contest, the Women's National Book Association Annual Writing Contest, and the Bethlehem Writers Roundtable Short Story Contest. I am

an avid collector of mystery novels and am proud of my nearly complete Agatha Christie collection.

Lynette Esposito
Lynette G. Esposito, MA Rutgers, has been published in *Poetry Quarterly*, *North of Oxford*, *Twin Decades*, *Remembered Arts*, *Reader's Digest*, *US1*, and others. She was married to Attilio Esposito and lives with eight rescued muses in Southern New Jersey.

Robert Eversmann
Robert Eversmann works for *Deep Overstock*.

Joe Galván
Joe Galván is a writer, artist, composer and anthropologist. He was born in Harlingen, Texas, in the Rio Grande Valley of Texas. His work has appeared in *Texas Monthly*, *The Believer*, *Buckman*, *Deep Overstock*, *1001*, and *Barrelhouse*. He lives in Portland, Oregon.

Gabby Gilliam
Gabby Gilliam is a writer, an aspiring teacher, and a mom. She lives in the DC metro area with her husband and son. Her poetry has appeared in *One Art*, *Anti-Heroin Chic*, *The Ekphrastic Review*, *Vermillion*, *Deep Overstock*, *Spank the Carp*, and others. Her fiction has appeared in *Grim & Gilded* and multiple anthologies. You can find her online at gabbygilliam.com or on Facebook at www.facebook.com/GabbyGilliamAuthor.

Ken Gosse
Ken Gosse prefers writing short, rhymed verse with traditional meter and generally full of humor. First published in *The First Literary Review–East* in November 2016, since then in *Pure Slush*, *Lothlorien Poetry Journal*, *Academy of the Heart and Mind*, and others. Raised in the Chicago suburbs, now retired, he and his wife have lived in Mesa, AZ, over twenty years, usually rescue cats and dogs underfoot.

Cynthia Graae
Cynthia Graae's fiction, creative nonfiction, and poetry translations have appeared or will soon appear in online and in print publications, including the *Garfield Lake Review*, *Persimmon Tree*, *Alternate Route*, *Griffel*, *Barren Magazine*, *North Dakota Quarterly*, *The Common Dispatches*, *Kinder Link*, *Maine Character Energy*, *Exsolutas Press*, *Canadian Women Studies*, *Maine Public*, *HuffPost*, *The LA Review*, and *Exchanges*. She lives in New York City and Hiram, Maine.

SARAH DAS GUPTA
Sarah Das Gupta is a retired English teacher from near Cambridge, UK. She taught in India, Tanzania as well as the UK. As the head of department, she was often charged with overseeing the English section of the School Library and purchasing books.In most schools she was also responsible for stocking class libraries. She started writing this year after an accident which kept her in hospital. Her work has been published in many magazines from twelve countries, including US, UK, Australia, Canada, India, Germany, Croatia and Romania. Writing has given her the challenge and drive to learn to walk again.

HEATHER HAMBLEY
Heather is a Latin teacher turned translator. She has a BA in Classics from Reed College, where she developed a deep passion for Latin poetry and mythological women, especially Helen of Troy. She currently lives in Central Oregon with her husband Andy and their 15yo doggo Mo. She loves horror movies, particularly anything cozy or campy. Her dream is to translate Latin in the horror space, so hit her up with your spells, spooks, and spoofs. Heather's website is latinklub.wordpress.com.

ANN HOWELLS
Ann Howells edited *Illya's Honey* for eighteen years. Recent books are: *So Long As We Speak Their Names* (Kelsay Books, 2019) and *Painting the Pinwheel Sky* (Assure Press, 2020). Chapbooks include: *Black Crow in Flight*, Editor's Choice in *Main Street Rag*'s 2007 competition and *Softly Beating Wings*, 2017 William D. Barney Chapbook Competition winner (Blackbead Books). Her work appears in small press and university publications including *Plainsongs*, *Schuylkill Valley Journal*, and *San Pedro River Review*. Ann is a multiple Pushcart nominee and has been named a "Distinguished Poet of Dallas" by the Dallas Library.

VALERIE HUNTER
Valerie Hunter worked at her college library as an undergrad, where she occasionally read the new acquisitions when she should have been shelving. She now teaches high school English and maintains a classroom library with a sadly low circulation rate. Her poems have appeared in publications including *Room Magazine*, *Wizards in Space*, and *Frost Meadow Review*.

RJ EQUALITY INGRAM
RJ Equality Ingram lives in Portland, Oregon & works as a used bookseller for Goodwill Industries of the Columbia Willamette. RJ received their MFA in creative writing from Saint Mary's College of California. RJ's first

collection of poetry *The Autobiography of Nancy Drew* is forthcoming from White Stag Publishing. RJ's cat Brenda lost a leg haunting a house on a hill.

ALETHA IRBY
My name is Aletha Irby and I have been writing poetry for over fifty years. My personal library includes books of poetry, mysteries, ghost stories, novels, and histories. My work has been published in *Main Street Rag, Lady Blue Literary Arts Journal, VOLT, Shot Glass Journal, Palo Alto Review, Tiny Lights Online*, and many other journals. I am very grateful to have been granted this time, on this planet, to spend with the English language.

S.Z. JAMES
Ben Norman (AKA S.Z. James) is a college student and bookseller/barista at Powell's City of Books. He is currently "hard at work" on his second novel.

IVY JONG
Ivy Jong (she/they) is a queer writer focused on Classics and Greek myth. She is a bookseller at Powell's City of Books in Portland, Oregon.

GURUPREET K. KHALSA
Gurupreet K. Khalsa considers connections, space, time, cosmic flow, reality, illusion, and possibility. Her work has appeared in *The Poet, TL;DR Press, New York Quarterly, Far Side Review, Necro Productions, IHRAF Publishers, aurora journal, Written Tales, Last Leaves, Delta Poetry Review, Ricochet Review, Mocking Owl Roost, Pure Slush*, and other online and print publications, Multiple poems have received awards. She is a current resident of Mobile, Alabama, having lived previously in Ohio, Washington State, India, New Mexico, and California. She holds a Ph.D. in Instructional Design and when she's not floating about in space, she is a part time instructor in graduate education programs.

J. REMY LESTRANGE
I work at the Powell's Books warehouse, in the call center. I've worked here for nine years. I take calls about books all day, answering inquiries about stock and arranging orders for our phone guests. I also spend a little time in the back of the warehouse, unboxing used book buybacks and processing them for a new home on our shelves. I delight in discovering what a box holds, and to touch and smell each little volume of previously loved pulp. To pass it along to be loved by others, adopted and read again and rediscovered by those who are unaware they need it until it's leering longingly at them from the aisles, is a treasure.

Kara McMullen
Kara McMullen is a writer and research scientist based in Portland, Oregon. Her work has appeared in *Diagram*, *The Normal School*, and elsewhere. She is the steward of a large collection of books, many of them in French.

Keith Melton
Mr. Melton holds a Master's in City Planning from Georgia Tech and a BA in Economics and International Studies from the American University. His work has appeared in numerous publications including *Amethyst*, *Compass Rose*, *The Galway Review*, *Big City Lit*, *Confrontation*, *Kansas Quarterly*, *Mississippi Review*, *The Miscellany*, *Cosmic Daffodil*, *Grand Little Things*, *Plum Tree Tavern*, *Siren's Call* and others.

Karla Linn Merrifield
Karla Linn Merrifield has had 1000+ poems appear in dozens of journals and anthologies. She has 16 books to her credit. Following her 2018 *Psyche's Scroll* (Poetry Box Select) is the full-length book *Athabaskan Fractal: Poems of the Far North* from Cirque Press. Her newest poetry collection, *My Body the Guitar*, nominated for the 2022 National Book Award, was inspired by famous guitarists and their guitars and published by Before Your Quiet Eyes Publications Holograph Series (Rochester, NY). She is a frequent contributor to *The Songs of Eretz Poetry Review*. Web site: https://www.karlalinnmerrifield.org/; blog at https://karlalinnmerrifield.wordpress.com/; Tweet @LinnMerrifiel; https://www.facebook.com/karlalinn.merrifield.

James B. Nicola
James B. Nicola is a returning contributor. The latest three of his eight full-length poetry collections are *Fires of Heaven: Poems of Faith and Sense*, *Turns & Twists*, and *Natural Tendencies* (just out). His nonfiction book *Playing the Audience* won a *Choice* magazine award. He has received a Dana Literary Award, two *Willow Review* awards, *Storyteller's* People's Choice magazine award, one Best of Net, one Rhysling, and ten Pushcart nominations—for which he feels both stunned and grateful. A graduate of Yale, James hosts the Writers' Round Table at his library branch in Manhattan: walk-ins are always welcome.

Timothy Arliss OBrien
Timothy Arliss OBrien (he/they) is an interdisciplinary artist in music composition, writing, and visual art. He has premiered music from opera to film scores to electronic ambient projects. He has published several books of poetry, (*The Queer Revolt*, *The Art of Learning to Fly*, & *Happy LGBTQ Wrath Month*), and is a poetry editor for *Deep Overstock*, a judge for Reedsy

Prompts, and a poetry reader for *Okay Donkey*. He also founded the podcast & small press publishing house, The Poet Heroic, and the digital magic space The Healers Coven. He also showcases his psychedelic makeup skills as the phenomenal drag queen Tabitha Acidz.
Check out more at his website: www.timothyarlissobrien.com

MOLLY O'DELL
My first good job was a librarian during college. I loved looking at the books and shelving them. I never had any notion I'd become a writer because I was hell bent on going to medical school which I did. After practicing medicine for some years, I discovered that growing through reading and writing was as important as mastering the myriad of medical topics required to be a good physician. I eventually received an MFA and have published poems and essays as well as three books. More at www.doctormolly.net

JANIS LEE SCOTT
Janis Lee Scott is an author from the San Joaquin Valley. She now lives in Oregon, writing and painting cows and lighthouses. She is a writer, a mother, a grandmother, and a volunteer. She is the official album artist for up-and-coming country and western star Reverend Shane.

JIHYE SHIN
Jihye Shin is a Korean-American poet and bookseller based in Florida.

A.A. SLATERPRYCE
A.A. Slaterpryce worked at Potsdam Public Library until this summer, connecting people with books of all kinds & deepening his relationship with the community. It was magical, to share the love of books between close friends and town strangers. It made him appreciate the diversity of perceptions given to us by the kinds of books we read. After exploring those creative realms of written imagination in Northern New York, A.A. Slaterpryce now pursues possibilities of language & communication on the hills above an Adirondack lake. They find movement in music when struggling to write, & seek the source of life in delicious home-cooked dishes.

SOPHIA SPISAK
Sophia Spisak used to volunteer to act as Fischer the Raccoon, a library mascot in Fort Collins, Colorado. The suit was really hot and you had to stuff ice packs down your shirt to survive in there. Now she lives in Portland and makes art occasionally. She hopes to one day be a mascot again.

Coleman Stevenson

Coleman Stevenson is the author of *Breakfast: 43 Poems* (Reprobate/GobQ Books, 2015), *The Accidental Rarefication of Pattern #5609* (Bedouin Books, 2012), *The Dark Exact Tarot Guide,* and a book of essays accompanying the card game Metaphysik. Her writing has also appeared in a variety of journals and anthologies, and she is a regular contributor for tarot.com.

Her fine art work, exhibited in galleries around the Pacific Northwest, focuses on the intersections between image and text. She has been a guest curator for various gallery spaces in the Portland, Oregon area, and has taught poetry, design theory, and cultural studies at a number of different institutions there, most currently for the Literary Arts Delve series, which includes seminars at the Portland Art Museum.

Z.B. Wagman

Z.B. Wagman is an editor for the *Deep Overstock Literary Journal* and a co-host of the Deep Overstock Fiction podcast. When not writing or editing he can be found behind the desk at the Beaverton City Library, where he finds much inspiration.

Mike Wilson

Mike Wilson's work has appeared in magazines including *Amsterdam Quarterly*, *Mud Season Review*, *The Pettigru Review*, *Still: The Journal*, *The Coachella Review*, and in Mike's book, *Arranging Deck Chairs on the Titanic*, (Rabbit House Press, 2020), political poetry for a post-truth world. He resides in Lexington, Kentucky, and can be found at mikewilsonwriter.com

Nicholas Yandell

Nicholas Yandell is a composer, who sometimes creates with words instead of sound. In those cases, he usually ends up with fiction and occasionally poetry. He also paints and draws, and often all these activities become combined, because they're really not all that different from each other, and it's all just art right?

When not working on creative projects, Nick works as a bookseller at Powell's Books in Portland, Oregon, where he enjoys being surrounded by a wealth of knowledge, as well as working and interacting with creatively stimulating people. He has a website where he displays his creations; it's nicholasyandell.com. Check it out!

All rights to the works contained in this journal belong to their respective authors. Any ideas or beliefs presented by these authors do not necessarily reflect the ideas or beliefs held by Deep Overstock's *editors.*

Printed in the USA
CPSIA information can be obtained
at www.ICGtesting.com
JSHW081057241223
54270JS00004B/189